GHOSTS
BENEATH
OUR FEET

**Other Apple® Paperbacks by
Betty Ren Wright**

The Dollhouse Murders
The Secret Window
Getting Rid of Marjorie

GHOSTS BENEATH OUR FEET

Betty Ren Wright

AN
APPLE®
PAPERBACK

SCHOLASTIC INC.
New York Toronto London Auckland Sydney

ISBN 0-590-40755-4

Copyright © 1984 by Betty Ren Wright. All rights reserved. Published by Scholastic Inc., 730 Broadway, New York, NY 10003, by arrangement with Holiday House, Inc.

12 11 10 9 8 7 6 5 4 3   7 8 9/8 0 1/9

Printed in the U.S.A.   28

For my grandparents,
and for Aunt Bertha
and Uncle Joe

Chapter One

The bus smelled of stale sandwiches and gasoline, the air-conditioning had failed two hours ago, and Katie Blaine felt better than she had in months. Milwaukee was behind them, and she, her mother, and her stepbrother had a long, healing summer ahead. *We're going to be okay now,* Katie told herself. *In Newquay.* Even the name sounded right, a good place in which to start over.

Her mother sat next to the window, her eyes closed. A bag of chocolate kisses lay on the magazine she'd been reading. Cautiously, Katie shifted the bag to her own lap and helped herself to three candies. The chocolates were just going to waste, melting in the sun. She crumpled up the silver wrappings and licked her fingers, her head down so no one would see.

"Don't you ever stop eating, kid?" Jay's words from

3

across the aisle slapped Katie in the face. She turned to make sure her mother hadn't heard. Why did Jay have to be so nasty? After two years of sharing the same parents, the same apartment—the same life!—he still wouldn't miss a chance to insult her.

Annoyed with herself for blushing, Katie stuck out her tongue, but she was too late. Jay's shaggy blond head had bent again over his science-fiction paperback. He'd been reading ever since they left Milwaukee.

Think about something happy, Katie ordered herself. *Think about Newquay.* She pictured for the hundredth time what it would be like. There would be a town square—most little towns had a square, didn't they?—with tall trees and a library and a courthouse and a little white church and a general store. Maybe a candy store, too, with pink-cheeked ladies selling chocolates made from an old family recipe. And a fountain in the middle of the square. And a bandshell! Yes, there would definitely be a bandshell.

"Honestly, Kate!" Mrs. Blaine sat up and reached for the bag of candy. "I bought these in case we had a long wait between rest stops. I didn't expect you to stuff yourself! Do you know how many calories there are in just one chocolate?"

Katie sighed. She didn't want to know. "I've only had a few," she protested. "They're melting."

Mrs. Blaine twisted the top and dropped the sack to the floor. "Probably not fit to eat," she said. "Oh, my, it's so hot in here. And the heat makes me sleepy." With a sudden change of mood, she slipped an arm around

Katie's shoulders and hugged her. "Not much longer, hon. When we get to Uncle Frank's, we'll have a good supper and relax. I bet it'll be cool in Newquay, at least at night. After all, we'll be four hundred miles north of Milwaukee."

"Does he live near the middle of town?" A red brick house with white shutters would be perfect. Or maybe a white house with pillars.

"Who knows? When he wrote asking us to come, it was the first time I'd heard from him in years. He must have been desperate for help, or he wouldn't have asked, I'm sure." Her mother took a tissue from her handbag and patted her forehead. "When I was your age, he used to come to Milwaukee on business once in a while, and he always stayed with us. Grandpa Traynor was his best friend. I remember that he was gentle and sweet in those days, and he brought me little presents. But you've heard all that before." Mrs. Blaine leaned back and closed her eyes. Her face sagged into its familiar sad expression. "So sleepy," she whispered, and almost at once her breathing became deep and regular. Ever since Katie's stepfather, Tom Blaine, had died eight months ago, her mother would often hurry off to sleep, as if eager to get away.

Feeling deserted, Katie looked around and saw that Jay had closed his book. "Jay?" She decided to forgive him for being mean about the chocolates. It was important to start out right when they arrived in Newquay. But he seemed lost in his thoughts. His straight nose and heavy brows reminded her of his father's face.

"Hey." She slid out of her seat and settled herself on Jay's armrest. "Did you finish the book?"

"Yup."

"Was it good?"

"Fair." For just a moment his expression softened. Maybe he guessed how hard she was trying.

"We're going to be there pretty soon. In Newquay."

"Big deal."

"You know what? I have this very peculiar feeling that I've been to Newquay before. In another life, maybe. I know just what it's going to be like. Maybe it's because I've always wanted to live in a small town. Haven't you?"

Jay's blue eyes narrowed. "I've always wanted to stay in Milwaukee where I belong. I've never felt like racing off to the end of the earth just because some old guy I don't even know says he needs help. But then, no one asked what *I* wanted to do."

It would be easier if he'd shout instead of speaking with such icy calm. Katie could take care of herself in a shouting match. But he acted as if she wasn't important enough to fight with. He'd rather just lean back and wait for her to stop bothering him.

The fat man in the seat next to Jay looked as if he enjoyed listening to people be rude to each other. His smirk made Jay's coldness unbearable.

"Well, I don't care what you think!" Katie snapped. "I'm really glad we're going to be in a nice little town all summer, and I'm going to have lots of friends there. You could, too, if you gave people half a chance!" She swung back across the aisle into her own seat.

If only Tom Blaine were here right now . . . but, of course, if Tom were alive they wouldn't be on their way to Newquay. Katie's mother wouldn't be thinking about a job; there would be no depressing memories to run away from. If Tom were alive, they'd be going on weekend trips to the Mississippi or to Green Lake this summer. They'd be swimming and fishing. Katie might be learning to water-ski. As long as Tom was alive they'd been a family, and there had been days and even weeks when Jay seemed to accept his new mother and sister. He'd teased Katie, the way other brothers teased their sisters, and they'd groaned at each other's jokes. But Tom's death left Jay lonely and bitter just as his mother's death had eight years before. "I don't need anybody," he'd told Katie when she tried to comfort him the day of the funeral. "Don't worry, I can take care of myself."

"What were you and Jay arguing about just now?" Her mother whispered the words without opening her eyes. Katie realized she hadn't been asleep after all.

"Nothing important."

"Poor kid, he's furious because he had to leave those unappetizing friends of his." She kept her voice very low. "I just hope he won't sulk all summer and upset Uncle Frank.

"Better use your comb," she went on. "We should be arriving in a few minutes." Mrs. Blaine smoothed back her own straight brown hair and adjusted the clasps that held it in a knot low on her neck.

Katie scrabbled through her shoulder bag for a comb, one eye on the scene flashing by the dusty windows.

There was a tiny single-pump gas station, a supper club built of shiny yellow logs, and then a row of clapboard cabins set back under tall trees. Over and beyond the scattered buildings the northern Michigan forest loomed, as it had for many miles. Columns of white birch and aspen marched against dark evergreens. Purple, yellow, and orange wildflowers decked the roadside.

"It's really pretty," Katie said. "Don't you think it's pretty, Mom?"

Mrs. Blaine nodded. "I guess so. I'm a city girl myself. I doubt that I could get used to such wild, lonely country on a permanent basis. But I'm sure it will be fine for a couple of months."

"Sure, it will," Katie said. "It'll be terrific! You know what I think? I think it's going to be like living on a movie set. We'll get to know everybody in town, and we'll shop in the general store and take walks around the square and—"

She stopped as the bus made a lurching turn off the main highway and started up a sloping blacktop road. Small shingled houses were scattered along either side. Between cluttered yards were fields dotted with sheds and abandoned cars. A faded sign pointed a wooden finger ahead.

"'Newquay,'" Katie read. "We're finally here." Jay glowered at her, and the fat man next to him smirked again.

"At last," Mrs. Blaine said. And then she gasped, "Oh, dear!"

Katie looked out at gaping storefronts, fading signs,

and crumbling sidewalks. Most of the rusty-looking, red-painted buildings appeared deserted; the few that were occupied had a dreary and desolate look. With a feeling close to panic, Katie peered across the aisle. More deserted buildings, including a couple that seemed close to collapse. The bus jolted from side to side on the narrow street, missing some of the worst potholes and shuddering through others. At last it stopped, and the front door wheezed open, letting in a blast of hot air.

The fat man was watching Katie's face. "Regular garden spot, ain't it?" he teased. "Not what you expected, huh? This old town's dead as a doornail—has been for years."

Katie was stunned. "Where's the square?" she whispered. "Where are the trees and the bandshell and the little white church? Oh, Mom, this can't be Newquay. It can't be!"

Mrs. Blaine patted Katie's arm. "Never mind," she said weakly. "So it isn't what you expected. Or what I expected, for that matter. What's the difference? We won't be here forever."

Katie stared at her. She wanted to say, "How can we begin our new life in a place like this? How can we start fresh in a town that's dead?" But she couldn't get out any words at all.

Chapter Two

"What now?" Katie asked. They stood on the sidewalk, their suitcases at their feet, in an ovenlike heat that stole their energy and breath. The bus started up with a snort and a grumble.

"I suppose we'd better ask directions to Uncle Frank's house," Mrs. Blaine said finally. "Maybe in there. . . ." She nodded toward the nearest storefront. BUS STATION was hand-lettered over a poster in the window, and next to it was a smaller sign: UNITED STATES POST OFFICE. The poster showed a bus zipping along beside water that had long ago faded to gray. "Jay, would you . . . ?"

He shrugged and started toward the door.

"I'll go, too," Katie said. Anything was better than standing outside, looking at Newquay.

A tiny middle-aged woman stood behind a counter

10

sorting mail. In spite of primly waved hair and thick glasses, she looked like a little girl playing postmistress. Her eyes were bright with curiosity as she examined Katie and Jay.

"If you've come to pick up mail, you'll have to show identification," she announced. "I don't take anybody's word. This post office is just the same as the U.S. government." She waited, daring them to deny it.

"We're looking for Frank Pendarra's house," Jay said. "Do you know where he lives?"

The woman ignored the question. "You're the family, then," she said. "Come to take care of the poor soul. Well, it's easy to see the resemblance. You've got the Pendarra nose," she said, focusing her nearsighted gaze on Jay, "and you've got his eyes, missy."

"But we're not even—" Katie began.

"Didn't know Frank had any relatives left, till it got out that he sent for help. About time you got here, that's what I say. Poor soul is *sick*. Ornery, too. Bein' sick gets the old ones that way. My mother, now, she was the meanest—"

"Yes, ma'am," Jay said. "Can you tell us where Frank lives?"

"Of course I can." She sounded annoyed. "I can't do my job 'less I know where people live, can I? I certainly can tell you two are brother and sister. Can't miss it. I can spot a family likeness every time."

Jay made a queer choking sound, and Katie realized he was fighting laughter, as she was. Even though she wanted Jay for her brother, she couldn't pretend they looked alike. He was tall, skinny, and fair; she was shorter than most of her friends, and rounder, too, with dark brown hair.

"We can take Frank's mail to him," Jay suggested slyly. "If we can find his house, that is."

"That's easy enough. Just go down to the corner and then straight up the hill. Get to the top and keep going. Big and gray, that's the Pendarra place. He doesn't have any letters. You can tell him Mrs. Trewartha said hello and how-are-ye."

Katie bobbed her head. "Is there a bus going that way?" she asked. She was pretty sure she knew the answer, but she dreaded a long uphill walk with heavy suitcases.

"Bus?" Mrs. Trewartha repeated. "Can tell you're from the city, all right. The only bus Newquay ever sees is the one you folks just got out of. Wouldn't know what to do with a bus if we had one, I'm sure. Walking's good for you," she added.

Jay followed Katie out into the sun. Without a word he picked up two suitcases, and Katie took the third, leaving her mother the two shopping bags. Mrs. Blaine hurried after them. When they stopped again, beyond the dusty windows of the bus station—post office and grinned at each other, she stared at them in astonishment.

"What in the world . . .?"

"The lady in the post office." Katie giggled. "She says she could tell Jay and I are brother and sister because we look so much alike."

"And we both look like our uncle Frank," Jay finished. His smile faded, as if he'd suddenly remembered how much he didn't want to be here. "Silly woman," he snorted and picked up the suitcases. He sounded disgusted, but there was a twitching at the corners of his mouth, as if the smile were struggling to return. *Maybe things really will be different here,* Katie told herself. *Even if it's a dead town, like that awful man said.*

They turned the corner and faced the steepest hill Katie had ever seen—a baby mountain, with a ragged sidewalk that gave way to patches of weeds every fifty feet or so. Old houses with drooping porches and sparsely curtained windows alternated with vacant lots full of buttercups and rubbish. The gravel road was red, as if the ground itself were rusty.

"This is iron country." Mrs. Blaine's explanation came in little puffs. "Or it used to be, before the mines were emptied and closed up. I suppose that's why the houses are red, too—with so much dust, it saves repainting them every couple of years."

Katie doubted that these houses had ever been re-painted. Each step made her dream of pretty little picture-book Newquay more ridiculous. And it was so hot! Who would have thought it could get this warm in a town surrounded by tall green woods and only fifty miles or so from the deep waters of Lake Superior?

They trudged on. "I hope you have those directions right," Mrs. Blaine panted. "I couldn't climb another hill after this one."

"The whole stupid town's on one hill," Jay snapped. "So how could anybody make a mistake?"

"Oh, Jay, for goodness' sake—" Mrs. Blaine's voice

was oddly thin. Katie glanced at her mother and saw her
stagger. Her shoulders were bent under the weight of the
overstuffed shopping bags.

"Are you okay, Mom?"

Abruptly, Mrs. Blaine sat down on the sidewalk.

"Mom!" Katie squeaked with alarm. She knelt and put
an arm around her mother. "What's the matter with you?"

Mrs. Blaine leaned forward. "I'll—I'll be all right in
a minute," she said. "It's just the heat . . . and this terrible
hill . . . and everything."

Katie looked around frantically. "I'm going to get some
water," she told Jay. "You stay here."

They had stopped in front of a narrow red house with
a deep porch. The front door hung open. Katie dropped
her suitcase and ran up the walk.

"Is anybody home? Please! Is someone here?"

There was a movement at the end of a dim hallway,
and a girl appeared.

"Who's there?"

The girl was about Katie's age, tall and leggy. She
wore blue jeans and a man's shirt, and the hair on one
side of her head was piled high in fat sausage curls. The
rest of it hung to her shoulders.

"What do you want?"

"My mother needs some water. She fainted—sort of.
Out in front of your house."

The girl turned and disappeared. Katie went down the
hall into a large, cluttered kitchen. The girl was at the
sink filling a glass.

"You 'ere to look after Frank?" The cracked voice made

Katie jump. A tiny old woman sat in a corner close to the huge gas range. She was dressed in black, and in spite of the heat she wore a scarf knotted tightly under her chin. Sparkling dark eyes peered out of a face as round and creased as a dried apple.

"Yes." Katie reached for the water the girl offered her.

"Well, you tell Frank for me, they're goin' to get out, no matter what," the old woman said. "You can't stop 'em, my dear, and neither can I. Nobody can."

The words meant nothing to Katie. "Thanks for the water," she said and dashed back down the hall.

"You tell Frank what I said, missy." The cracked voice followed her. "You tell 'im!"

Mrs. Blaine had moved from the sidewalk to the scruffy patch of grass in front of the house. Jay had put two of the suitcases behind her, and she sat leaning against them, her eyes closed. When Katie pressed the glass to her mother's lips, she drank eagerly.

"Thanks, hon."

"You can bring her inside if you want to."

Katie looked up and saw that the girl had followed her out of the house. In the afternoon sun her up-and-down hair gleamed like copper.

"Mom, do you want to—"

But Mrs. Blaine struggled to her feet, brushing away their helping hands. A little color had returned to her cheeks. "I'm all right now," she said. "Really. That was very silly of me. Thank you, anyway." She looked up the hill. "We're nearly to the top now, aren't we?"

"I'll carry the shopping bags the rest of the way." Katie

hurried to pick them up before her mother could protest. "I can do it, honest." She lifted the suitcase in her other hand, and Jay picked up the remaining two. He still hadn't spoken, but he was looking at the tall girl as if she were an alien just arrived from Mars.

"Oh, gosh, my hair." The girl raised a hand and touched the lopsided curls. "I was trying something new," she said, her face flaming. "I bet I look—"

She didn't finish. Jay's expression told her quite clearly how she looked.

"Your hair is really pretty," Katie said. "I love red hair." But the girl's lips tightened, and she didn't answer. Jay started up the hill, and Mrs. Blaine followed with a wan smile. Katie hesitated, longing to patch things up.

"That lady in the kitchen—"

"My grandma." The girl sounded hostile.

"She knew we were going to Frank Pendarra's house. I guess in a small town everybody knows what's going on." The words sounded critical, as if Katie were accusing the townspeople of being nosy. "What I mean is, what did your grandma mean for me to tell him? What was she talking about?"

"I don't know." The girl turned her back and stalked up the narrow walk to the house. "She says things sometimes. Just forget it." She went into the house and slammed the door behind her.

Katie bit her lip. They hadn't even gotten around to introducing themselves. She sighed and started walking. Darn that Jay, anyway. He could make trouble without saying a word. It was too hot and she was too uncomfortable to tell him what she thought right now, but she promised herself she'd do it later. He'd spoiled her chance to make a friend.

As they neared the top of the hill, the houses were farther apart. At the crest, both the town and the sidewalk ended. The red gravel road, deeply rutted and edged with dandelions, stretched ahead of them across a meadow and into a wide stand of trees.

Jay dropped the suitcases and sat on one of them. Mrs. Blaine huddled on the other. "This is the dumbest thing I ever heard of!" he exclaimed. "An empty field. That woman in the post office must be laughing—"

"That's enough." Mrs. Blaine wiped her face. "We're all in danger of heatstroke, and complaining won't help. You go along the road a way, Katie, and see if there are more houses beyond those trees. We'll wait here."

With a worried glance at her mother, Katie trotted away. Small white butterflies rose in front of her, lifted like flower petals by the warm wind. Far off to the left, pointed red hills marched in a line and vanished beyond the woods.

At the edge of the woods, Katie hesitated. The road ahead was like a tunnel edged with pines and clusters of bone-white birch. Bears could be lurking among those trees. Or wolves! The leafy walls seemed to close around her as she forced herself to go on.

She rounded a turn, just in time to catch a movement on the path. A deer bounded in front of her. It came and went so swiftly that she had only a glimpse of its flowing grace. Then she was alone again, breathless with pleasure.

She'd seen a deer! Even Jay would have to be impressed when he heard that.

Two more curves, and the little wood ended as abruptly as it had begun. Another meadow lay beyond it, this one dotted with willows that hung limp in the heat like sagging umbrellas. Partly hidden by the trees was a tall gray house with a porch around its front and one side. Shutters hung at angles next to the windows, and bushes crowded around the porch. Except for a sturdy stone chimney, the whole place looked as if it might cave in at any minute.

Someone was sitting in a chair close to the front door. As Katie stared, the figure rose, and she saw that it was an old man. He tottered to the edge of the porch steps and raised a hand over his head. She couldn't tell whether he was waving a greeting or shaking his fist.

"You, girl!" The old voice was harsh. "You come 'ere. Come 'ere, I say!"

Katie stepped back into the deepening shadows. She couldn't stop herself from retreating. Not that house, she thought. Not that man, with ragged, shoulder-length hair and an angry bark of a voice. This couldn't be the end of their long journey.

Katie turned and raced back through the woods, trying to think what she'd say to her tired mother.

I found the house.

I saw Uncle Frank.

And then perhaps the words that had been pounding

through her head from the first moment she'd looked out the bus window at Newquay's main street. *Jay's right. We shouldn't have come to this place. Let's go back to Milwaukee right now.*

Chapter Three

"An old feller could starve 'ere by 'imself, 'e could!"
Settled again in his rocking chair on the porch, Uncle
Frank had hardly stopped talking since the Blaines arrived. "Yesterday I called down to the town for a bit of
bread and some soup, and they 'aven't brung it yet. That's
why I 'ollered at you, girlie. Wanted you to take word.
Tell 'em to 'urry up."

Katie sat on the front steps, obeying her mother's sug-
gestion that she "keep Uncle Frank company while I look
around." Keeping him company, Katie decided, meant
keeping still. The long white hair grew increasingly un-
ruly as Uncle Frank combed it with gnarled fingers, his
thin frame trembling. It was surprising that someone who
looked so fragile could complain so loudly.

In spite of the stream of words tumbling around her,

Katie was lonely in the fading light. The woods loomed dark beyond the meadow, and the willows close to the house formed great tents of shadow. Milwaukee and her friends seemed ten thousand miles away.

Her thoughts went back to the dark, shrunken grandmother in the house halfway down the hill. What was it she'd said? *You tell Frank they're goin' to get out, no matter what. You can't stop 'em.... Nobody can.* Katie wished Uncle Frank would calm down a little so she could ask him if he knew what the message meant.

"You'll 'ave to go down 'ill to the store, girlie. There's nothing to eat in this 'ouse." The old man slapped the arm of his chair, and Katie jumped. "What's your name, then?"

"Katie. Katherine Jane Carson Blaine."

"Well, you and that boy can go—what's 'is name again?"

"Jay. He's my stepbrother, Uncle Frank. He's upstairs—lying down, I guess. He's sort of tired." She wanted to apologize for the cool way Jay had acknowledged Mrs. Blaine's introductions. "He'll feel better tomorrow."

"Don't care about that." Skinny arms flailed the air. "You two 'ave to go back down the 'ill and get food. Better start right now."

The front door opened, and Katie sighed with relief as her mother came out onto the porch. Mrs. Blaine looked cheerful. This was what they'd come to Newquay for, Katie realized—for a job that would keep her mother too busy to grieve. The worse things looked at Uncle Frank's house, the better her mother was going to like it.

"No one has to go to the store tonight," Mrs. Blaine said. "There are several cans on the cupboard shelves, Uncle Frank. We can make do until tomorrow."

Katie thought Uncle Frank looked disappointed. "Delivery boy from the store 'id 'em, then," he muttered. "I looked, but I couldn't find anything to eat. Not a bite."

"He probably thought he was being helpful." Mrs. Blaine stood at the top of the steps and looked out over the yard. If she found the view depressing, her smile didn't waver. "It's nearly five," she said. "We'll have supper in a little while. You run along, Katie. I want to talk to Uncle Frank."

Katie jumped up. "I'm going to unpack my stuff," she said.

The paneled foyer was bigger than her cozy bedroom at home. A grandfather clock six feet tall towered against one wall, its pendulum stilled. Beyond it a stairway rose into shadows, and on the opposite wall double doors led into a long parlor that looked as if no one had sat in it for years.

On tiptoe, Katie followed a hallway that opened into a dining room. Beyond that was the kitchen, with a wide table covered with oilcloth, painted cupboards, a pantry, a gas range, and—wonder of wonders—an old-fashioned wood-burning stove. Katie unlatched the oven door and stared into a sooty cavern, feeling like the witch in *Hansel and Gretel*.

The kitchen shades were drawn, and the air was hot and musty. Katie closed the oven and went back to the dining room, then turned off through partially opened French doors into a small library. *At least I'll have plenty to read,* she told herself and ran a finger across rows of bindings. But the books did little to cheer her. The house felt neglected, unloved—and what else? She had a strange feeling that something was about to happen. Here in the middle of a meadow on the edge of a forgotten town, the house seemed to be full of secrets.

Upstairs, a dim corridor divided the second floor in half. Katie turned toward the first open door, then stopped, startled by a movement at the end of the hall. Someone was there! Someone short and dark-haired, wearing jeans and a T-shirt. Katie took a quivery breath. What a place for a full-length mirror! She'd have to remember it was there, or she'd scare herself every time she came upstairs.

Her mother's suitcase stood, unopened, in the large front bedroom. Katie's bag was in the smaller room next to it. There was a lumpy-looking bed, a dresser with a wavy mirror, and a bedside stand. The blue rug was furred with dust, and the rosebud wallpaper was peeling at the corners. Katie opened the two windows and pushed back graying curtains to let in some air.

Jay appeared in the doorway. "There's no TV in this dump," he announced. "How're you going to like being stuck in the middle of nowhere without a television set?"

Katie's heart sank. She'd miss television a lot, but not as much as Jay would.

"Listen." He threw himself on the bed and groaned at the unyielding mattress. "Could you talk to her—to your mother?" Katie saw that he was very serious. "This whole thing isn't going to work. We don't belong here—anybody can see that. The old guy doesn't seem so sick to me, and besides, he isn't even related to your mother. Why does she think she has to come running when he says he needs a nurse? It doesn't make sense."

Katie sat carefully in a rocker with a split in its cane seat.

"Frank was just like a real uncle to Mom a long time ago," she said. "And he's not supposed to live by himself anymore. The doctors told him—"

"He must have a family of his own somewhere."

Katie shook her head. They'd been over all this when Uncle Frank's letter arrived. "He had a son who was killed in an accident when Mom was a little girl. And his wife died a long time before that. After the son was killed, Uncle Frank changed a lot, Mom said. I guess he was really bitter. He wrote a few times, but he never came to Milwaukee again."

Jay sat up. "He could go to a nursing home. Lots of people do."

"Maybe he will, later on," Katie said. "But he'd like to stay in his own house as long as he can. And you know Mom wanted to get away from Milwaukee this summer—"

"Well, I didn't!" Jay punched a pillow and then sneezed as dust rose around him. "We were going to fix up Doug Krocker's motorbike and do a lot of other good stuff." He looked at Katie intently. *"You* don't want to stay here, do you? Tell the truth."

Katie turned away. "I—I don't know," she said finally.

"It isn't the way I thought it would be, but I don't see how we can leave Uncle Frank now."

She smiled, willing him to smile, too. "Maybe you'll have fun here," she coaxed. "You don't know yet. We might as well find out what it's like, now that we're here."

"No way." Jay clenched his fists. "I just may go home by myself."

"You can't!"

"Want to bet? Stay here and suffocate if you want, kiddo. I'll make my own plans!"

The conversation was over. No more brother-and-sister talk. Katie leaned back in the rocking chair as he stomped out of the room. She winced as the door slammed behind him with a bang that shook the walls.

Chapter Four

After all his concern about starving, Uncle Frank barely touched the soup and fruit Katie's mother served for supper. He was like a sad old scarecrow, sitting there half asleep. Even Jay must see that he was sick.

Mrs. Blaine had a notepad next to her plate. "The first thing we have to do is clean house," she said. "You two can do your own rooms tomorrow and then give me some help downstairs. The whole place needs an airing."

"Housework, ugh!" Katie looked sideways at Jay, who ignored her. "Not all day, Mom! I want to find out if there are any kids living near here." There was one, she knew—the girl they'd met on the hill—though she probably wasn't interested in becoming a friend.

"You'll have time for that, too," Mrs. Blaine assured her. "After you do a little cleaning." She looked at Jay.

"Come on, Jay, why so grim? What's on your mind?"

Jay stared at his plate. Katie squirmed.

"I'm not asking you to work all the time, you know," Mrs. Blaine continued. "I want you to have fun this summer. Get outside—explore—enjoy yourself. A new place can be exciting."

Jay nodded and sipped his soup.

Uncle Frank's spoon clattered to his plate.

"He's asleep," Katie whispered. "Mom, he hardly ate anything at all."

Mrs. Blaine touched Uncle Frank's arm, and the shaggy white head jerked. "Would you like to go to bed now?" she asked gently. "If you aren't hungry, I can fix you a snack later on."

He looked around the table as if he'd forgotten who they were. "Tired," he mumbled. He pushed back his chair, and Mrs. Blaine hurried to help him up.

What would it be like to be old, tired, confused, to be always on the outside of what was happening? Suddenly Katie remembered the question she'd wanted to ask Uncle Frank earlier. Here was something interesting that only he could tell her.

"Uncle Frank, we met a friend of yours when we were on our way up here. She's a teeny-tiny old lady, and she lives partway up the hill."

The old man grunted. "Nancy Trelawny. Came over from Cornwall with 'er folks same year as me. Been in that 'ouse ever since, she 'as."

"Well, she sent you a message," Katie hurried on. "She said to tell you 'They're going to get out,' and she said,

'You can't stop them.' What did she mean, Uncle Frank?"

The old man straightened, and the deep-set brown eyes blazed with anger and disgust.

"Lot of Old Country nonsense, that's what," he snapped. "I won't listen to such talk, you 'ear me?" Then his shoulders sagged. "She's a crazy woman, that Nancy," he said. "Talks foolishness—always did. Don't pay her any mind." He shuffled out of the kitchen with Mrs. Blaine close behind him, her face stiff with disapproval at Katie's probing.

"What do you think of that?" Katie demanded as soon as they were out of earshot. "Did you see how excited he got when I told him what that old lady said?"

Jay looked bored. "So he's right—she's a crazy woman."

"But he knew what she meant!" Katie exclaimed. She brushed a strand of dark hair from her face. "Didn't you even notice that? He knew what Mrs. Trelawny was talking about, and it really got to him. He didn't like it one bit."

"So?"

"So this is the only exciting thing that's happened since we got off that bus," Katie retorted. "It's a real mystery!" She leaned back and considered. "Maybe Uncle Frank and Nancy Trelawny were lovers when they were young. Maybe they quarreled and married other people, but she never stopped loving him, and now she wants to warn him that something bad is going to happen."

"And maybe you're crazy, too," Jay said. "That doesn't sound like a love message to me—more like a threat."

He looked at her with amusement and disdain. "What a dreamer! Never a dull moment with you around!"

"What's wrong with that?"

"Nothing, I guess." Jay grinned, and for a while they sat quietly in the dusk. Then Jay shrugged. "The thing is, you make up problems for the fun of it," he said. "You don't have any real ones."

His tone suggested that he had worries she knew nothing about. Katie waited, hoping he'd say more, but he pushed back his chair and stood up. "See you," he muttered.

Katie finished her canned pears, spooning the sweet syrup slowly to make it last. A mystery, she thought. Jay could tease all he wanted, but a mystery would make up for having to spend the summer in this dreary place.

She checked to see if there was one last pear half in the can, then crossed the kitchen to the open back door. This was the right setting for a mystery, no question about that. A small porch extended from the house like a raft afloat on a sea of meadow grass. Katie went down the steps, stopping on the last one to gaze into the twilight. There were probably rabbits and mice and all kinds of wild creatures living in this field. Even snakes! She pulled her foot back hastily, and as she did, her toe caught in a rotting board and she lost her balance. One moment she'd been looking out over the meadow. The next, she was stretched full-length on the ground. Her chest ached with the force of her fall.

She started to get up, then froze. There was a groaning beneath her, a somber sound that began and ended in seconds. She lifted her head to look around, then pressed her ear to the ground once more. Silence. But as she lay there, not moving, the earth shuddered beneath her hands.

Katie scrambled to her feet and flew up the porch steps. She hurtled through the door just as Mrs. Blaine returned to the kitchen.

"Katie, for heaven's sake! Uncle Frank's trying to sleep." She sank into a chair. "You really disturbed him just now," she went on, without noticing her daughter's flushed face. "I don't want any more questions about mysterious messages, okay? Uncle Frank's heart is weak. He needs rest and quiet and *no stress*."

Katie peeked over her shoulder at the open door. She half expected to see something horrible hulking there.

"And where's Jay?" Mrs. Blaine asked. "He's going to have to watch his tongue, too."

"He went upstairs." Katie took a deep breath to steady herself. "I'll wash the dishes."

She couldn't tell her mother what had happened. Not now, anyway. In the first place, her mother probably wouldn't believe her. And in the second place, she already had a sick old man and a rebellious stepson to worry about. She wouldn't want to hear that there was a Mysterious Something moving around under Uncle Frank's backyard.

Chapter Five

"You're one very flaky kid. Period." Jay scrambled to his feet and brushed bits of grass from his hair. "I don't hear anything. Except bees buzzing."

Katie collapsed on the bottom step of the porch. "Well, you would have heard something really scary last night," she snapped. "And I'm not flaky! I did hear a noise underground, right where you were lying. And I felt the earth shake, too!"

"Katie," Mrs. Blaine called from inside the house. "Finish making your bed, and you can call it a day. What are you doing out there, anyway?"

Katie stood up and shook the bedspread she was supposed to be airing. "Want to go for a hike later on? We might see a deer."

"I don't know. Maybe."

31

Katie sighed. She'd waited all morning for a chance to tell Jay what had happened the evening before, and now he didn't believe her. She frowned as she went back into the house. Was it possible that she'd imagined the sound deep in the earth? And the tremor? She had to admit that in the harsh light of day the whole experience seemed unreal.

Her mother sat at the dining room table making out a grocery list. She looked tired but contented after their morning's work. The freshly vacuumed rug was several shades brighter, and the room smelled of lemon oil. Uncle Frank, propped up in a chair, looked better, too. His hair was combed, and his face shone as if it had been scrubbed with one of Mrs. Blaine's brushes. A bright-colored afghan was folded over his knees. He avoided Katie's eyes and watched Mrs. Blaine warily.

"I'm going down the hill to do the shopping myself," Mrs. Blaine said. "It's not nearly so warm today, and I want to see what the store has to offer. I'll bring back a few things for dinner tonight, and the rest can be delivered tomorrow. What would you like, Uncle Frank?"

Uncle Frank looked startled. "Don't matter. Anything'll do for me."

"But there must be something you'd particularly enjoy."

The old man considered. "Don't suppose you can make pasties," he said glumly.

"Pasties? I've heard of them, but—"

"Never you mind, then. Ain't no use if you only 'eard of 'em. There's a trick to doin' it right."

"It's a Cornish dish, isn't it?" Mrs. Blaine asked.

"Yup. You take meat and taters and onions and beggies—"

"Beggies?"

"Root-a-bag-as." He drawled each syllable. "Should think you'd 'eard of *them*, if you've 'eard of pasties." He paused. "I could eat a bit of chicken, maybe," he offered in a friendlier tone.

Mrs. Blaine sounded relieved. "Roast chicken it'll be, then. Katie and Jay like it, too." She looked sharply at Katie. "Where's your brother?"

"Outside. Looking around."

A worry line shaped itself between her mother's brows. "Are you two going to do something together this afternoon?"

"I don't know. We might go for a hike."

"That sounds like fun."

Fun was unlikely, but if Jay would just go with her, Katie would be satisfied. Otherwise he'd be up in his bedroom plotting how to get back to Milwaukee.

"This place is really nowhere," he told Katie later on, when she suggested the hike again. "Absolute zero!" But he fell into step beside her, and he looked as eagerly as she did for wildlife in the little woods between Uncle Frank's house and town. *Come on out, deer*, Katie pleaded. She longed for something pleasant—anything!—to make Jay hate Newquay a little less.

But no deer appeared. As soon as they reached the open meadow on the other side of the woods, Jay began to hang back.

"Let's just go to the top of the hill," Katie coaxed. "I want to see if it's as steep as it seemed yesterday."

It was. The red-gravel road and the ragged sidewalk unrolled like shabby ribbons at their feet. Halfway down, in front of the house where Nancy Trelawny and her family lived, blue-jeaned figures were playing catch.

"If they miss, they'll have to chase the ball all the way to the bottom of the hill," Katie marveled. "Some fun!"

"Who cares about the ball game? Look at the machine!"

Jay pointed across the street. Leaning against a sagging front porch was a massive black motorcycle. Its gleaming perfection looked out of place.

"Come on," Jay ordered. "I want a close-up look."

Katie followed gladly. When they were almost opposite the motorcycle, the front door of the house opened, and a lanky boy in jeans and a black T-shirt came out. His glance touched the Blaines and moved away.

"Wait here," Jay said. "I'm going to talk to him." He ambled across the road, kicking up tiny red dust-devils at every step.

Katie watched him, hardly daring to hope. Maybe Jay and the cycle's owner would become friends. If that happened, Jay might stop thinking about going back to Milwaukee.

One of the ball players dropped out of the game and threw herself on the crumbling curb, legs outstretched. It was Nancy Trelawny's granddaughter. Today the red-gold hair hung smoothly except for a single narrow braid. She swung her head back and peeked at Katie over her shoulder.

Across the road, Jay was deep in talk with the boy in the black T-shirt. Katie knew her stepbrother had forgotten she existed. She started down the hill, stepping over the biggest cracks in the sidewalk and detouring around a three-wheeled wagon that had been abandoned where it fell apart. The girl watched her coming.

"Hi. I'm Katie Blaine. Thanks for helping us yesterday."

"It wasn't anything." The girl's voice was cool. "Your mother okay?"

"She's fine." Katie sat on the curb and wrapped her arms around her knees. "It was so hot yesterday, and this hill is pretty steep if you aren't used to it."

"You're from out of town." The girl said it like an accusation.

"Milwaukee. I don't know anybody in Newquay." Katie tried to sound offhand and failed. She decided to be frank. "It's kind of lonesome—you know?"

The girl's expression softened a little. "I'm Joan Trelawny. Your stuck-up brother likes motorcycles, huh?"

"More than anything. He'll probably talk that boy into giving him a ride."

"No chance," Joan said. "Skip Poldeen doesn't give rides. He thinks he's king of the hill, he does." She swung around to face Katie, and her face was transformed by the warmest of smiles. "Are you going to stay in Newquay? If you want, I can show you where things are. The library's real small, but they get lots of paperback romances. Tuesday Lake is about a mile from here, and the beach is pretty nice. And there're movies in the Con-

solidated High School gym two nights a week." Now the
wary look returned. "I bet that sounds stupid to you—
movies in a gym."

"Oh, no! Maybe we can go together sometime. We're
going to be here all summer."

"Your stuck-up brother would say it was stupid,
though." Joan jumped to her feet and cocked her head,
imitating Jay. "Say there, kid," she drawled, "does everybody wear their hair in that weird way in this stupid
town?"

Katie giggled and changed the subject. "Are those your
brothers and sisters playing ball?"

"The skinny boy is my brother Ed, and the redhead is
my sister Lillian. The other kids are my cousins. Baby
Patty—she's in the house with Ma and Gram. And I have
a sister who's married in Hancock and a brother in the
Navy. My dad works at the lumberyard." Joan stopped
for breath. "How many are there in your family?"

"You saw them all yesterday," Katie said. She watched
Skip Poldeen wheel the motorcycle out to the street with
Jay trailing close behind. "There's my mom, of course,
and Jay's my stepbrother. My real dad died when I was
a baby, and my stepfather—that was Jay's dad—died
last fall."

"How about Frank Pendarra? Isn't he your uncle?"

Katie explained that Uncle Frank was a family friend,
not a real uncle.

"Only three people in a family," Joan mused. Clearly
she couldn't imagine what that would be like. "When
you have turkey, I bet you can always get a drumstick—

hey, look there!" She stared in astonishment as Skip Poldeen mounted the motorcycle and Jay climbed on behind
him. The engine snarled. Then the big machine took off
in a wide U-turn and hurtled down the hill. The ball
players scattered with angry shouts.

"You see?" Katie said. "I knew he'd get a ride."

"I never saw old Skip let anybody else on his precious
machine," Joan said. "I guess he wants to show off for
the big-city kid. Mostly he yells at us to get away if we
even look at it. He's bad news."

"What do you mean, bad news?"

Joan shrugged. "Sort of wild. Want to come in and
have a Coke?"

Katie followed her into the house. She wanted to hear
more about Skip Poldeen, and she wanted to talk to Joan's
grandmother again. If Uncle Frank wouldn't tell her the
meaning of the strange message, maybe she could find
it out for herself.

The living room looked far too small to hold all the
Trelawnys Joan had listed. A huge couch, two overstuffed
chairs, a television set, and a long coffee table crowded
with framed photographs took up most of the floor space.
The dining room was full of furniture, too, but the kitchen
was spacious and bright. Katie had hardly looked around
during her quick visit the day before. Now she saw Joan's
tall, round-cheeked mother rolling out dough on the table,
with a redheaded baby perched at her elbow. One tiny
pink foot rested on the pastry board.

"Pleased to meet you," Mrs. Trelawny said. "We heard
you was comin' to Newquay—glad someone is up there

on the hill with old Frank. Poor feller shouldn't be alone. Get your friend a cold drink, Joanie. There'll be fresh Cousin Jacks in a little while." She chuckled at Katie's expression. "Cousin Jack is what we call a Cornishman *and* what we call his favorite cookies, too. Every Cousin Jack loves Cousin Jacks. You ask old Frank if they don't." She picked up a glass and thumped it into the dough, making a neat two-inch circle.

"Did ye tell Frank what I said, girlie?" Katie turned to Nancy Trelawny, who sat in her corner next to the stove. The legs of her chair had been cut down to accommodate her own short limbs, so that she seemed to be crouching on the floor. "Did ye tell 'im they was still at it?"

"I told him," Katie said. "But I don't know who you meant."

"Knackers." Joan spoke the word as if it explained everything. "Gram worries about 'em all the time. She says they're getting meaner now."

"What's a knacker?"

Joan took two bottles of Coke from the huge, old-fashioned refrigerator and handed one to Katie. "Knackers are"—she paused, as if expecting Katie to laugh—"knackers are evil ghosts that live in a mine. When miners get killed underground, sometimes their spirits stay in the mine, and they keep digging and knocking on the tunnel walls, trying to escape. Gram says the knackers in Newquay mine are restless 'cause it's nearly thirty years since the big accident." She tilted her chin at Katie. "I'll bet you think this is silly."

"Joanie." Mrs. Trelawny was reproving. "No reason

to be saucy about it, I'm sure. Most people don't believe in knackers. Who's to say what's the truth, anyway?" She slid a spatula under a circle of dough and transferred it to a cookie sheet. "Gram came to this country from Cornwall when she was a girl. Her folks believed in knackers, so she did, too."

Gram Trelawny's black eyes sparkled. "You listen to what I tell you, girlie," she ordered. "They be down there, to be sure. Ugly little devils with squintin' eyes and gapin' mouths. Diggin' under this very 'ill, they are, and full of rage 'cause they can't get out. Longin' to make mischief—"

Katie gasped. Her drink slipped from her fingers and crashed to the floor. Cola rippled across the worn linoleum.

"Oh, I'm sorry!"

Joan snatched a towel from a rack over the sink and began mopping up the stream. "That's okay," she said. "I'll get you another bottle."

"See there, Gram?" Mrs. Trelawny exclaimed. "You've gone and scared Joanie's friend. You and your evil spirits. Just look at that white face." She squeezed Katie's shoulder with a floury hand. "It's all Old Country tales, girl. Gram and Joan are a couple of biddies when it comes to tellin' ghost stories. Don't you believe 'em."

"But—But I do believe them!" Katie croaked. She was so excited she could hardly speak. "I believe there really are knackers, Mrs. Trelawny. There must be. You see, I heard them myself last night. Right under Uncle Frank's backyard!"

Chapter Six

Baby Patty cooed, breaking the silence in the kitchen.

"You're making that up," Joan said. "You shouldn't tease Gram."

"I'm not," Katie protested. "I heard the knackers last night. Honest!"

"You didn't!"

"Now, now," Mrs. Trelawny scolded, "if Katie thinks she heard something—"

"Oh, she 'eard 'em, all right!" Gram Trelawny's eyes shone, and she clapped her hands like a child. "You're a good girl," she said. "A fine girl! You 'eard 'em in Frank's backyard, you say?"

"Yes." Joan glared, and Katie began to wish she'd kept still. "I didn't know what it was—I thought it might be

40

the beginning of an earthquake. There was a sound—
like a groan—"

"Yes, yes," Gram encouraged her. "That's it! Digging
right up to Frank's place, they are. The boy wants to go
'ome, poor chap."

"Gram!" Now Joan's mother looked disturbed, too.

"What boy?" Katie asked. "Who do you mean?"

"Frank's boy, of course. Kenneth, his name was. Buried in the mine accident thirty years gone, and 'e's been
down there ever since. I could feel it—I knew 'im and
'is mates was close to breakin' out. Thirty years of diggin', an' now it's goin' to happen. You tell Frank—"

"Oh, no," Katie groaned. "I didn't know Uncle Frank's
son died in the mine. That's terrible!" She remembered
the old man's face when she'd delivered Nancy Trelawny's message the night before. He hated what she'd
said, and why shouldn't he? The very idea of a beloved
son killed and then changed into an evil spirit who kept
struggling to get back to the surface. . . . Katie shuddered.
"Poor Uncle Frank."

Gram Trelawny struggled to her feet. "It'll 'appen soon,
mind my words," she said. "The knackers'll get out! Bad
mischief's comin'—I can feel it."

To Katie's frightened eyes Gram looked as if she were
in a trance. Her fists were clenched at her sides, and she
stared past the two girls and through them. Mrs. Trelawny
hurried to the old lady's side and guided her back to her
chair.

"Now, Gram," she soothed her, "you know nothing's
goin' to happen. Don't get yourself all stirred up. The

girls are just goin' for a walk"—she shot Joan and Katie a glance—"and you don't want to spoil it for them, do you? That's a dear."

Still clutching their Coke bottles, the girls scuttled down the hall to the porch. A moment later Joan's mother joined them at the door.

"Our Gram's an old lady," she told Katie. "She always did like her bit of excitement, and she doesn't get much of it anymore. So she makes her own, you might say. You mustn't mind her stories."

But Katie couldn't stop thinking about the pain she'd caused. "Uncle Frank must have heard that story about his son and the knackers before," she said. "He got angry when I told him what Gram said."

"Yes, he's heard it. Our Gram's had this in her head for months, and she won't let it go. Ever since she realized the mine accident happened thirty years ago this summer. Right after Frank came home from the hospital, she went up to his place when we weren't watchin'—just slipped off one afternoon—and warned him there was trouble comin'. Got no thanks for it, you may be sure, but she don't discourage easy, bless her." Mrs. Trelawny gave Katie a sharp look. "She's a good woman, Katie. The old tales make life more interesting for her, that's all. She needs 'em." She turned back into the house, and soon the girls could hear her talking softly in the kitchen.

"Still," Joan kicked the porch railing, "if you hadn't said you really heard the knackers, Gram wouldn't have gotten all upset. I like the spooky stories she tells, but I don't pretend to really believe 'em."

"I wasn't pretending," Katie protested. "I did hear something. If it wasn't knackers, what was it? You'd believe, too, if you'd been there." Katie looked down the hill, hoping to see Skip Poldeen's motorcycle come around the corner. She wanted to go home right away and tell Uncle Frank she was sorry she'd hurt him. She'd never, never deliver another message without knowing exactly what it meant.

"Skip's probably racing all around the county," Joan said, following her glance. "He'll be trying to scare your brother." She eyed Katie thoughtfully, then seemed to make up her mind. "If you want to go for a walk, it's all right with me."

They put their empty Coke bottles next to the door and started up the hill, scuffing their feet and thinking their separate thoughts as they climbed.

At the top of the hill, Joan turned to the left and led the way along a strip of crumbling fence. Ahead of them the tall grass rippled like water in the breeze. Below, Newquay baked on its hillside, the dull red of the houses broken by tiny patches of grass and bright spots of red and blue and yellow laundry hung out to dry.

"When my dad was a kid, this was a pretty town," Joan said. "He said it was like a picture on a calendar."

Katie picked a buttercup and tied a knot in its stem. "It looks really nice from up here," she said. "Not so—"

"Not such a mess," Joan finished for her. "I know what you're thinking. In the old days the Newquay mining company owned the whole town, and they took care of things. There were lots of little towns like Newquay around—mining locations, they called 'em. But after the accident, the company said the ore was almost gone anyway, and it would cost a ton of money to open up the mine again. It wasn't worth it. So they sold the houses cheap to the people who lived in 'em and just pulled out. My dad was only fifteen then, but he had to go to work in the lumberyard to help support his family. And since then it's mostly the old people who stick around here." She pointed across the fields at the conical red hills Katie had noticed yesterday. "Those are slag heaps left from the mine—waste stuff. The shaft house is just beyond them—you can see the tip of the tower from here."

Katie took a deep breath of the green-smelling air and began to feel better. She could see the calendar-picture Newquay as clearly as if she'd been there. It was as pretty as the Newquay she'd imagined on the bus.

"I like it up here in the meadow," she said. "If I lived here, I think I'd come here every day."

"If you lived here, you'd want to move away," Joan said. "Same as I'm going to, when I get out of school." Her voice softened as she looked down at the town. "Sure, I'll miss home, and I won't go to some big, dirty city, you can bet. I'll find a nice small town that has jobs and lots of people my own age."

Far below them, a motorcycle growled.

"Here they come," Joan said. "I guess you'll want to go back."

"I'd better," Katie agreed, but now she was sorry to cut their walk short. She promised herself she'd come back to the meadow soon.

When they reached the road, the motorcycle was just turning up the hill. It bucked and snorted from one side of the road to the other, leaving behind a zigzagging trail of dust until it stopped in front of Skip Poldeen's house. The boys jumped off, and Skip opened a saddlebag and took out a piece of cloth. He stood, arms folded and watching critically, while Jay began to wipe away the layer of dust that coated the black surface.

"Look at that, now." Joan's voice was heavy with scorn. "Skip's making him pay for the ride."

"Jay probably thinks it was worth it."

"I guess." Joan slowed her steps when they were opposite the boys. "If you're giving rides, I'll go next, *Mr*. Poldeen," she said. "But I won't be your slave afterward."

"You get near this machine and you'll be sorry." Skip Poldeen's voice was thin, and Katie realized that he wasn't much older than Jay. He looked from one girl to the other, and his lip curled. "What a pair!" he jeered. "A carrot-top and a tub of lard."

Joan took a step forward. "You take that back!"

Skip laughed unpleasantly. "Tomorrow at ten," he said to Jay, who had dropped the dust cloth and stood listening, his face bright red. "Be here if you want to go along. Don't make any difference to me."

Katie started up the hill, not wanting any of them to see the tears in her eyes. She wasn't a tub of lard, but she hated Skip Poldeen for saying the words. How could Jay stand to be around such a mean, cruel person?

"Hey, Katie." Joan was coming after her. "Want to go to the shaft house tomorrow? Gram says it's haunted."

"I don't know." Katie struggled to keep her voice steady. "I might have to help my mother."

"Don't pay any attention to that Skip." Joan's steps slowed. "He likes to hurt people's feelings."

"He didn't hurt mine," Katie lied. "Who cares what some hick says, anyway?"

The steps behind her stopped, and Katie trudged on alone. There. She'd done it. And she didn't care. She'd had enough of Newquay to last her for the whole summer.

She decided she'd spend the rest of the summer reading the books in Uncle Frank's library—every last one of them. And in September she'd go back to her friends in Milwaukee and never think about this town again.

At the top of the hill the wind was waiting to lift her hair and cool her cheeks. She walked more slowly toward the woods, wiping her eyes with the back of her hand.

"Wait a minute, will you?" Jay was calling. She didn't turn her head as he caught up to her.

"You should see that guy handle a cycle on the open road," he said. "He's terrific!"

"He's disgusting. I hate him."

Jay laughed uncomfortably. "Don't be so thin-skinned," he said. "Can't you take a little teasing?"

"I don't have to take anything from that jerk," Katie retorted. "He's not going to push me around."

"He doesn't push me around either. I offered to wipe off the bike."

"Wait'll Mom hears you went for a ride without wearing a helmet."

Jay's fingers dug into her arm, and they stopped to

face each other on the shadowy path. "Listen," he said, and there was a desperate note in his voice, "if you blab to your mother, I've had it with you and her and this town. The works! I can maybe have some fun with Skip— he's not half bad, whatever you think. You just keep still and mind your own business."

Katie shook off his hand and stalked on. Threats, she thought. Insults and threats. "I don't care what you do," she said in her coldest voice. "If you want to break your neck, go right ahead."

It was hard to believe that just twenty-four hours ago she'd thought this was the summer when they'd finally learn to be a loving, caring family.

Chapter Seven

Skip Poldeen streaked toward Katie on his motorcycle. The handlebars, pronged like a deer's antlers, loomed menacingly, and the engine's roar was the sound of a wild animal. Sobbing, Katie scooped up a rock and threw it straight at Skip's grinning face. But as the rock left her hand, the face over the handlebars changed, and it was Jay who thundered toward her. Katie screamed and threw herself to one side as the cycle passed in a rush of wind. She lay still, unable to move even though she could hear the tires squeal and knew he was turning around to come back. The ground began to tremble, and a groan welled up from the earth. . . .

With a gasp Katie sat up in bed. Where was she? What was happening? She fell back on her pillow and stared at the ceiling. "It was just a dumb dream," she said out loud, but her palms were wet. She could still feel that terrifying tremor beneath her and hear the motorcycle's roar. *Another neat thing about this summer*, she thought bitterly. *Nightmares!* She couldn't remember ever having a nightmare at home.

The sounds of a country morning were all around her. Birds chirped and whistled and piped, insects hummed, and there was a chirring sound that was probably a squirrel or a chipmunk.

From behind Jay's closed door came the wail of his favorite Beatles tape. Katie walked down the hall to the bathroom, watching the girl in the mirror move toward her. Was the mirror-girl a little thinner today? Katie *felt* thinner, no matter what Skip Poldeen said. She always felt sort of thin and wispy when she was depressed.

Downstairs, she found her mother fixing a tray for Uncle Frank, who was still in bed in his little room behind the parlor.

"Is he okay?" Katie asked anxiously.

Mrs. Blaine sliced toast in neat triangles. "Better, I think," she said, "though he doesn't say much. I'm sure he's relieved to have company here. He thought he'd improve as soon as he got home from the hospital, but living alone was just too much for him. He's a man with a lot of sad memories."

Katie poured cereal into a bowl and reached for the milk. "What're you going to clean today?" she asked. "I can help if you want me to."

Mrs. Blaine raised an eyebrow. "No cleaning today, thank you. As soon as the store delivers what I ordered yesterday afternoon, I'm going to start baking. Bread, cake, maybe a pie, lots of cookies. Uncle Frank has gotten out of the habit of eating much, and I want to see what I can do to tempt his appetite. I won't need any help, but it's nice of you to offer. Why don't you spend some time with your new friend? Or you and Jay can do something together. Is he still in bed?"

"His door's closed." The telephone rang, and Katie hurried to answer it. She didn't want to talk about Joan, or about Jay either.

"Hi. This is Trelawny, your hick friend on the hill."

Katie gulped, trying to decide whether the voice sounded angry.

"You know, the carrot-top."

Katie leaned against the wall. "This is—this is the tub of lard," she said, her voice cracking over the painful words. "I didn't mean what I said yesterday—"

"Do you want to go to the shaft house?" Joan demanded, brushing aside the apology. "Or we can hike out to Tuesday Lake, if you'd rather."

"The shaft house," Katie said. "If you're sure it's really and truly haunted."

"It is. Really and truly. You can ask Gram. I'll meet you at the top of the hill."

Katie dashed back to the kitchen. All of a sudden she felt like dancing.

"Maybe I can use some help after all," her mother said slyly. "You look a lot more energetic than you did before that phone call."

"I *am* energetic," Katie said. "Joan and I are going exploring."

"Will Jay go with you?"

Some of the good feeling slid away. "I don't think he'll want to. He'll have things to do."

"Like what?"

Katie finished her cereal and carried the bowl to the sink. "I don't know. He made a friend yesterday, too."

"Somebody nice?"

"I don't *know!*" Katie exploded. "I hardly met him."

"Well, you don't have to be so touchy about it. Just go along and have fun. I'm not being nosy, you know. I want this to be a good summer for all of us."

"I know." Katie gave her mother a hug and went outside, before the questions could start again.

The sky was overcast, and the breeze carried a promise of rain. Katie hesitated at the bottom step of the porch, and then, after a quick look over her shoulder to be sure her mother wasn't looking, she knelt and pressed her ear to the ground.

Silence. Not a shiver. Not a sound. Could she have imagined the tremor that first night? Jay's taunts and Joan's disbelief were more real to her now than Gram Trelawny's knackers. *Maybe I'm like Gram,* she thought as she brushed off her jeans and started around the house. *Maybe I just imagine things because I need a little excitement.*

Up close, the slag-heap hills were drab and dusty, their red slopes rutted by rain and dotted with weeds. Beyond them was the shaft house, and a cluster of low buildings surrounded it.

"It's like a monster tombstone," Katie said softly. "No wonder Gram says it's haunted."

Joan cocked her head. "It *is* a tombstone," she said. "A tombstone for all those men that died in the accident. I think there were sixteen of them. Two levels of the mine were flooded after the explosion—that's why no one even tried to get the bodies out." Joan led the way around a heap of rusty metal. "Come on. We should get inside the shaft house before it rains."

Thunderheads were piling up above the trees that bordered the mine property. It was perfect weather for ghost-watching. As the first drops of rain splatted on the red gravel, Joan started to run. At the back of the shaft house, she pointed at the nearest of several high windows.

"That's the one. Help me pull that crate over against the wall."

The rain beat down harder, and lightning carved angry streaks across the sky. Their faces streaming with water and their hair soaked, the girls pushed the big crate under the window, and Joan scrambled onto it. The window tilted when she pressed the lower pane, and she lifted her chin to the ledge.

"Okay—now push me!"

Katie pushed, and Joan swung upward through the opening. A moment later she leaned out of the window.

"Now hoist yourself up," she commanded. "I'll grab your shirt and pull." In no time they were both inside and climbing down off another crate that had been left just below the window.

"My brother Tom—he's the one in the Navy—taught me how to get in," Joan panted. "This place is supposed to be sealed up tight, but nobody can stop Tom." Her voice sounded hollow, as if they were at the bottom of a well.

Katie looked around nervously. The room had a high ceiling and was full of shadows. Along the sidewalls were a jumble of boxes and rusted tools. An ore car stood on narrow tracks in the center of the room, facing huge iron gates at the far end. Katie followed Joan toward the gates and stared in awe at the cables and chains dangling behind the bars.

"That's the shaft," Joan said. "Can you think what it was like to go down in the cage every morning—that's what they called the elevator thing—and not see the sun all day long? Ugh!"

Katie stepped closer to the gates. A chill breath came up from the darkness. She imagined some great beast crouched below, just out of sight.

"The rain's letting up," Joan said. "Good thing—otherwise we wouldn't be able to hear the ghosts."

Katie held her breath, wondering what she'd do if the machinery in the tower above them began to work and the cage rose into view. Faint, probably, or melt into a grease spot on the floor.

"Listen," Joan whispered. "Can you hear 'em?"

A low wail came from the mouth of the shaft. In spite of herself, Katie leaped back.

"Knackers!" Joan whispered. "Here they come!" She looked at Katie, wide-eyed. "The knackers are coming to get *us!*"

"That's wind in the shaft," Katie said uncertainly. "You know it is." Goose bumps popped up on her arms.

Joan made a sudden dash toward the crate beneath the window. "Let's get out of here before the cage comes up," she cried. "Those knackers could grab us and throw us down that shaft, and no one would ever know what happened." She hopped up onto the crate and lifted herself to the window ledge. "I'll go out first and catch you on the other side," she said. In a flash she'd swung her long legs over the side, and Katie was alone in the shaft house.

She scrambled onto the crate and reached for the sill. Even though she knew Joan was teasing, the shaft house was a very eerie place. She wanted to get out, fast.

Later, she couldn't even remember why she'd stopped to look over her shoulder. The wailing in the shaft had ended, but had she heard something else? A small sound, perhaps, almost like a sob, where there should be no sound at all? Whatever the reason, she turned and saw a movement in the shadows at one side of the shaft. As she stared, a white face framed in long blond hair became visible, and a pale hand lifted in the gloom. The figure moved forward with a strange hobbling motion, and the hand reached out.

Katie screamed. With one leap she was halfway through the window and dangling upside down on the other side.

"Wait!" Joan shouted and grabbed her shoulders. But Katie couldn't wait. Wiggling like a fish, she dropped over the sill, and both girls crashed to the ground.

Chapter Eight

"You're making that up!" The two girls faced each other from opposite sides of the crate. Joan wiped her face with the back of her hand, leaving a rusty smudge. "You know I was just kidding about the knackers. Now you're trying to get even. You think you can say anything and I'll believe it. Well, I don't!"

Katie's shoulder ached where she'd landed on it, and her knee was bleeding. She closed her eyes for a second and saw again the girl moving toward her with that strange bobbing gait.

"I'm not lying," she said. "I saw a girl's face with lots of blond hair, and a hand. Look for yourself."

Joan climbed up on the crate and reached for the sill. "Okay, I will," she snapped. "But I know you're making it up."

Moments later she was back on the ground. "There isn't anybody in there. The place is empty—the way it was when we went in."

"But she was there a couple of minutes ago. I saw her! Over in the corner close to the shaft."

Joan shrugged. Silently, the girls tugged the crate back to where they'd found it and started around the side of the shaft house. Thunder rumbled behind them, and the sky, which had seemed lighter for a while, darkened again. The mine buildings looked a thousand years old in the raw glare of lightning.

"We'd better hurry," Joan murmured. She brushed back her wet hair and started off.

"I'm telling you the truth," Katie said. "I hate it when people say I just imagine things."

"And I hate it when someone thinks I'm a *hick* who'll believe anything," Joan retorted. "You say you saw someone. I say you didn't. Let it go."

"I heard noises underground the first night we were in Newquay," Katie insisted. "I didn't make that up either."

They reached the meadow and waded through the grass, wind rising at their backs. At the top of Newquay hill Joan stopped. "I wasn't calling you a liar, Katie," she said. "It's just that . . . you *want* to believe in ghosts, right?"

"If I see them, I believe in them," Katie said. "And I don't think you're a hick, for Pete's sake. You aren't the only person who thinks I imagine things. My brother said I was flaky when I told him about the noise underground."

"Oh, him!" Joan's big laugh rang out, breaking the

tension. "Funny thing, me agreein' with him!" She began to run down the hill in great, galloping leaps. "So let's forget the whole thing," she called. "See you later, okay?"

"Okay." Katie turned toward the woods.

The rain began, and she threw back her head to catch the cool drops. Walking in summer rain had always been one of her favorite things to do. But then the drops turned to stinging needles, and thunder burst directly overhead. She began to run, racing light-footed through the woods, which seemed alive and full of movement as the storm closed in.

Katie called a hello to her mother in the kitchen and slipped upstairs to wash and change her clothes before lunch. She didn't want to answer questions about where she'd been and what she'd been doing.

But she needn't have worried. Mrs. Blaine's mind was on Jay. He'd left the house right after breakfast without a word.

"He's probably with his friend," Katie said cautiously. "I think they were going somewhere today."

"What's the friend like?" Mrs. Blaine studied Katie over her coffee cup.

"His name's Skip Poldeen. He lives across from Joan. I—I don't know what he's like. I hardly met him."

Her mother's lips tightened. "I can tell a lot from the look on your face," she said. "And I don't like what I see there."

"Maybe they're at Skip's house." Katie remembered her dream and pictured the motorcycle skidding up and down the rain-wet streets of Newquay. She glanced across the table at Uncle Frank, hoping for a distraction, but he was busy spitting watermelon seeds into his spoon. No help there.

The front door slammed, and quick steps sounded on the stairs.

"Jay?" her mother called.

After a defiant pause, the footsteps started back down. Jay came into the kitchen. His hair was soaked, and his shirt clung to his shoulders. He looked excited and a little scared. *The way I felt when I got home*, Katie thought. *Maybe he saw a ghost, too.*

"Where have you been?" Mrs. Blaine asked. "It worries me when you sneak away without a word."

"I didn't sneak. I just went." He *was* scared. Katie could hear it in his voice, see it in the way he kept glancing over his shoulder.

"Go upstairs and change," Mrs. Blaine said. "You're absolutely drenched. And then I want to hear about this Skip Poldeen."

Jay shot Katie a look of pure dislike.

"I have a right to know whom you're spending your time with," Mrs. Blaine insisted. "And I want to know where you go. I'm responsible for you, remember that."

Jay clenched his fists. "I can look after myself," he said, his voice squeaking out of control. "You don't have to be responsible for me. I'm not your kid!"

"You *are* my kid. Your father and I—"

"My father's dead! He's not part of this anymore—"

"'Ere, 'ere!" Uncle Frank's shout made them all jump.

"You're a saucy young feller, ain't you? We don't want such talk in this 'ouse, you 'ear? My boy Kenny never would have—"

Jay ran out of the kitchen. Katie got up to go after him, but her mother put out a hand.

"Let him be. He has to cool down."

"But he was *crying*, Mom! He doesn't mean all that stuff—"

"I said, let him go." Mrs. Blaine looked close to tears herself. "I'll talk to him later. You can clean up the lunch dishes, if you want to help. I'd like to lie down—"

The ring of the telephone cut her short. Mrs. Blaine hurried into the hall to answer it. Katie wondered if it was Joan, inviting her to come down the hill for the afternoon. She'd gladly walk through the storm to get away from the house for a while.

But when her mother returned, her face was white with shock. "That was the sheriff!" she exclaimed. "He wants to know if I have a son and if that son was home this morning." Katie waited, her heart thumping. "Two boys were seen running away from a cottage out at Tuesday Lake. They had forced a window to get inside and had taken some food. They got away on a motorcycle."

"Poldeen," Uncle Frank said. "Poldeen's got a motor-cycle."

Mrs. Blaine looked at Katie, who said nothing.

"'E'll come to no good, that Poldeen," Uncle Frank predicted. "Needs a whuppin', 'e does."

"Wh—what's going to happen?" Katie felt sick.

"I don't know. The sheriff said he'd be up here later

to talk to Jay." Mrs. Blaine sat down with a thump, as if her legs would no longer support her. "I should talk to him myself, but what if he runs off again and makes things worse? I don't know what to do. I just don't."

"You could whup 'im," Uncle Frank suggested. "I'd do it for ye, but 'e's a mite big." He stood up and stretched. "Time for my nap," he yawned. "Old feller like me can't take all this stirrin' up."

"Oh, Uncle Frank, I'm sorry."

The old man waved a dismissing hand. Katie decided that he wasn't as upset as he pretended to be. Maybe any kind of excitement was better than none at all. She remembered what Joan's mother had said: *The old tales make life more interesting for Gram. . . . She needs 'em.*

It looked as if the Blaines were giving Uncle Frank plenty to think about.

The thunderheads rolled away across the hills, and new ones took their place. The rain never stopped, a harsh downpour that threatened to drown the meadows around the house. Katie saw closed doors wherever she looked—Jay's, her mother's, Uncle Frank's. She thought of telephoning Joan but decided against it. Joan disliked Jay; she wouldn't understand why Katie felt sorry for him now.

She ended up in the library. It was the smallest and, in this weather, the darkest room in the house, but she switched on a lamp next to a massive chair of wood and leather and began pulling books from the shelves. There were some adventure series published fifty or sixty years ago. A row of biographies, in very small print, filled one shelf, and old textbooks crowded several others. There were lots of travel books and atlases. Katie finally chose *The Sinking of the Titanic*. The book jacket said it was a true story about a terrible disaster at sea. The subject suited her mood.

Two hours later she was completely lost in the terrible events of that long-ago night on the Atlantic. On the deck of the *Titanic*, John Jacob Astor was helping his wife into one of the last lifeboats, knowing they would never meet again on this earth. Katie's eyes blurred with tears. How dreadful it all was! Her own troubles seemed small by comparison. She could picture the listing ship, hear the brave men of the ship's orchestra playing "Nearer My God to Thee. . . ."

A car door slammed. A moment later there was a tapping, hardly louder than the rain.

Katie waited, hoping her mother would go to the door. When the tapping was repeated, she put her book aside and went down the hall. A tall figure waited on the other side of the screen. She opened the door for the visitor, who stamped his feet on the mat and mopped his face with a rumpled handkerchief.

"Enough rain to sink a ship," he said, making Katie wonder if he could read her mind. "I'm Sheriff Hesbruck. Mind if I come in?"

Katie stepped back. "I'm Katie Blaine. You can sit in the parlor if you want to. I'll call my mother."

"It's your brother I want to talk to," the sheriff said. He had a long, thin face, and eyes that studied her as if he intended to remember her forever. "That is, if Jay Blaine is your brother."

"My stepbrother. I'll get him. He's upstairs."

Was he going to arrest Jay? Her feet dragged as she climbed the stairs, and when she stood outside Jay's door, her voice was a queer, choky whisper. "Jay. Come on out. The sheriff wants to see you."

Her mother's door popped open as if she'd been waiting with her hand on the knob. Jay's door opened more slowly. They both stood looking at her, while thunder crashed overhead.

"What did you say?" Jay demanded. "Who wants to see me?"

"The sheriff. The sheriff's downstairs waiting."

Jay's face darkened, and he moved back into the safety of his room. Katie wished she could help him. John Jacob Astor must have looked a little like that, she thought, when he realized the *Titanic* was going down.

Chapter Nine

"Now what's going to happen?" The words had drummed through Katie's head all the time Sheriff Hesbruck, Jay, and Mrs. Blaine talked in the parlor. Now the sheriff was gone, Jay was back upstairs, Uncle Frank was still napping, and Katie and her mother were alone in the library.

"The sheriff let him off with a warning," Mrs. Blaine said, her voice flat and weary. "They didn't actually hurt the cottage, and the owner decided not to press charges. Jay says they went inside to get out of the rain."

"Then is everything okay?"

"No." Mrs. Blaine sat up. "No, everything is definitely not okay. I have a fifteen-year-old stepson who defies me and h-hates me"—her voice trembled—"and I don't know what to do about it. I know he misses his father terribly—so do I!—but there's no way I can take Tom's place. The four of us had such a short time before Tom died, that's the trouble." She shook her head at Katie's expression. "I shouldn't talk to you this way, hon—it's not your problem."

"It is too my problem," Katie protested. "We're a family."

"Some family!" Mrs. Blaine stood up and patted Katie's shoulder. "Oh, well, we'll get by," she said. "Don't worry, Katherine Jane. Right?"

"Right." As if you could stop worrying when you wanted to.

At the dinner table that evening Jay barely spoke, and even Uncle Frank seemed withdrawn. Mrs. Blaine urged everyone to have a second piece of raspberry pie, and she chattered about the storm and about the rainbow that had arced over Newquay when the clouds finally blew away. Katie listened through Jay's ears, and the words sounded empty, phony.

As soon as the table was cleared, Jay went back to his room and switched on a tape. Katie waited until her mother stepped outside to get some air, and then she hurried upstairs. When there was no reply to her knock, she opened Jay's door. The tape clicked off. He lay on the bed, staring at the ceiling.

"I'm sorry about today," Katie said.

"Thanks." Jay didn't look at her. "Not your problem."

"Whatever happened, I bet it was that Skip Poldeen's fault."

Jay swung his legs over the side of the bed and sat up. "Nothing happened," he growled, "nothing important.

And now I'm grounded for a whole week! And I'm not supposed to hang around with Skip anymore."

"I'm sorry," Katie said again. "I didn't tell Mom about him, except for his name."

"It doesn't matter. The guy who owned the cottage recognized Skip, and someone else told the sheriff I was with him. We didn't do any damage to the darned cottage—we were just trying to keep dry. Oh, and we opened a can of beans while we were waiting for the rain to stop. Big deal!"

"You were on somebody else's property. . . ."

"I know all that. I know it!" Jay sounded desperate. "Everybody says 'Enjoy yourself—have fun!' But when I do—forget it." His voice shook. "Your mother hates me."

Katie gasped. "She doesn't! That's an awful thing to say."

"Sure, she does. Why not? I'm nothing but trouble to her. She's stuck with me, right?"

"Wrong!" They stared at each other.

"One of these days," Jay continued unsteadily, "she's going to get fed up and tell me to get lost. You'll see. When she married my dad, I was just part of the package. Well, that's okay. I don't need anyone looking after me. I can just—"

There were tears in his eyes. Katie looked away, not wanting to see. This must be Jay's secret worry—the problem he'd hinted at that first night in Newquay. She longed to comfort him, but didn't know what to say.

She changed the subject. "Joan and I went to the mine

shaft house this morning. It's really a spooky place."

Jay cleared his throat. "So?"

"So it's really weird! When the wind blows a certain way, you can hear moaning and crying in the shaft. Joan says it's supposed to be the spirits of the miners who died down there."

Jay leaned back on his elbows, looking exhausted. "You're a goofy kid, you know that? Always hearing strange sounds! You've got a thing about underground ghosts."

"No, I haven't," Katie said. "But I did hear a noise in the backyard the other night, no matter what you think. The sounds in the shaft—well, that was just the wind, I know. There's something else, though." She hesitated, then plunged ahead. "Just as I was crawling out the window of the shaft house, I looked back and saw a girl watching me. She had long blond hair, and she put out her hand to me as if she wanted something."

"Another ghost, huh?"

"I don't know. Joan went back to look, but whatever-it-was was gone."

"It was probably one of the Newquay kids trying to scare the girl from the big city. You ought to write ghost stories—you've got the imagination for it." He leaned forward, suddenly intent. "Does your mother know you were in that shaft house?"

"No."

"Did she even ask where you went?"

"She knew Joan and I were going exploring."

"But not to the shaft house. You didn't tell her that.

You didn't tell her you broke into an old building with a hole in the floor a couple of thousand feet deep."

"Now, wait a minute," Katie protested. "It wasn't dangerous. There's a big iron gate in front of the shaft. And we didn't hurt anything."

Jay stood up and went to stare out the window. "The point is, she doesn't cross-examine you every time *you* go out the door. You were on somebody else's property as much as I was, but nobody hassled you about it. She doesn't *expect* you to get in trouble. Why is it I can't even turn around without getting yelled at?"

Because you do get in trouble, Katie cried silently. *And my mom never had a son before, and she's afraid of messing up*. But she knew there was some truth in what Jay said. Her mother did assume that Katie would behave herself, and that Jay wouldn't.

"You could try to show her she's wrong," Katie suggested timidly.

"You mean be a good boy and let her boss me around." He turned to her with an angry smile. "I've got one friend in this stupid town, and now I'm not supposed to see him anymore. He's the only person who isn't half dead—"

"Just because he rides a motorcycle!"

"That's part of it! I told you before—I hate this place. All I want is to go back to Milwaukee. But as long as I'm here, I'm going to have some fun, and nobody's going to stop me. Not the sheriff and not *her!*"

Katie wanted to slap him for that insulting *her*. "You're so dumb you don't know when people are trying to help you," she snapped. "You make me sick!" She marched out of the room and across the hall, trembling with rage.

Jay's voice followed her. "You're the one who's sick. You're psycho! I may be dumb, but at least I don't see spooks around every corner and hear 'em under every rock."

Mrs. Blaine came upstairs an hour later. By that time Katie was in bed. She didn't want to talk to her mother or to anyone else. She just wanted to be alone.

She heard her mother go down the hall to her room, then to the bathroom, then return to Katie's door. The knob turned, and Katie closed her eyes. After a moment the door clicked shut, and the footsteps retreated.

As the house became still, all the sounds of the summer night crowded in. An owl hooted, and insects banged against the screen. Far off, an airplane droned. Boards creaked. Katie tried to get to sleep, but sleep wouldn't come. Too much had happened today. The blond ghost-girl in the shaft house, the piercing eyes of the sheriff, Jay's fierce scowl—she saw them all when she closed her eyes.

Finally she gave up. *The Sinking of the Titanic* was down in the library; she might as well read if she couldn't sleep. She slipped out of bed and found the flashlight her mother had stowed in her dresser drawer "for emergencies." Then she opened the door and tiptoed into the hall.

The flashlight made a narrow tunnel of light. She waited for a minute to make sure no one had heard her, and then she started toward the stairs. As she moved, there was a shushing sound behind her, and a sudden chill in the air.

She whirled around, pointing the flashlight. There in the mirror at the end of the hall was the girl with the golden hair. As Katie stared, frozen, the girl took a hobbling step toward her and raised her hand.

Chapter Ten

The girl's eyes were sad, yet full of purpose. Even though her mother and Jay were only a few feet away, Katie felt as if she and the figure in the mirror were alone in the world. The girl's lips moved, and Katie strained for a message she couldn't hear. The words were important, but she couldn't understand them. The pale hand lifted in a sweeping motion, and the girl shook her head. Katie moaned in frustration.

"Katie!" Mrs. Blaine came out of her room. "What in the world are you doing? I thought you were sound asleep."

"I—I wanted to read for a while. My book is down in the library." Katie lowered the beam of light; the mirror was empty now except for her own reflection and her mother's.

"Well, you're heading in the wrong direction, dear

heart. Hurry on down if you must, but please do be quiet. Uncle Frank needs his rest."

Katie did as she was told. When she returned the hall was empty. Shakily she directed the flashlight at the mirror. Nothing. She went into her bedroom and closed the door.

Shadows retreated as she swung the flashlight in a slow circle, lingering longest on the mirror over the dresser. "I'm really sorry," she whispered into the dark. "I tried to understand, but I couldn't."

Now that she had time to think about what had happened, she felt more regret than fear. The ghost-girl had looked wistful, eager to communicate. Seeing her had been a shock, but as Katie climbed into bed, she found herself hoping the girl would appear again.

I've seen a ghost, she thought, full of wonder. *It doesn't matter what Joan says or Jay says—or anybody. It really happened! I've seen her twice, and she wants to tell me something. I'm going to lie here all night and figure out what it is.*

It was the last thought she had until morning.

When Katie went downstairs to breakfast, she half expected the others to notice a difference in her. Of course, no one would believe her if she told them about seeing the girl in the mirror—not her mother, fussing over Uncle Frank and coaxing him to drink all of his orange juice, and certainly not Jay, slumped in his chair, eyes down as usual. Katie didn't care. Something mysterious had happened between her and the girl in the mirror. The ghost had a message to tell, and she'd chosen Katie to help her.

Katie was washing the breakfast dishes and Uncle Frank was dozing over his coffee when Joan appeared at the back door.

"My ma says come for dinner with us this noon," she announced. "She said to tell you we're havin' star-gazzy pie."

"Having what?"

"Star-gazzy pie. It's Cornish. Ma says you should try it while you're in Newquay."

Katie motioned Joan to the table and poured two glasses of milk. She sat down, then jumped up again to fill a plate with the oatmeal cookies her mother had baked yesterday. "Why do they call it star-gazzy pie?" she asked. "That's a funny name."

"Funny dish, that's why," Uncle Frank muttered, rousing. "'Oo are you then, missy?"

"Joan. Joan Trelawny."

"Nancy's girl?" He peered at her.

"Her granddaughter."

"Well." He helped himself to a cookie and dunked it in his coffee. "I wouldn't put it past Nancy Trelawny to serve up star-gazzy pie at that," he said. "Always kept one foot in Old Country, she 'as." His face dimmed, as if he were remembering the message Gram had sent him.

"But what *is* it?" Katie demanded. "Somebody please tell me." She looked at Uncle Frank.

"These cookies are good," Joan said innocently. "I could eat 'em all."

"I'll tell ye what star-gazzy pie is," Uncle Frank offered. "My gram and 'er ma before 'er used to make 'em in Old Country when times was 'ard. Which they mostly were. Make a pie crust, you do, and put fish in it, and drop 'nother crust on top. Leave the 'eads and tails stickin' out, and them little eyes is just gazin' up—"

"At the stars!" Katie shuddered. "Star-gazzy pie! I've just decided I can't come for lunch. Thanks, anyway."

Joan giggled, and Uncle Frank actually smiled.

"If we don't have star-gazzy pie, will you come?" Joan asked. "I think my ma might change her mind. In fact, she's already making something else."

"I'll check." Katie ran upstairs to ask her mother. Jay's bedroom door was open, his bed neatly made.

"He's going to cut the grass around the house," Mrs. Blaine said. "I found a scythe in the basement yesterday, and there's a hand-powered mower in fairly good shape. He's grounded, you know," she added.

She listened absent-mindedly as Katie asked if she could go to the Trelawnys' for dinner.

"I guess so, hon. We'll miss you, but I'm glad you've found a nice friend." She looked again into Jay's room and sighed. "I just wish..."

Katie hugged her mother and ran back downstairs, unwilling to think anymore about how unhappy Jay was.

Ed Trelawny was as tall as Joan even though he was a year younger. He and Lillian, a small redheaded copy of her big sister, sat at the kitchen table and ate steadily, their eyes seldom leaving Katie's face. Mr. Trelawny, tall, sunburned, with thick gray brows over eyes as black as Gram's, watched her, too. She might have been uncomfortable, except that all three of them smiled whenever she looked at them.

"You never had pasties before then, missy," Mr. Trelawny commented during a pause in the girls' chatter. He looked down at the golden-brown pastry that nearly filled his plate, trying to imagine what a world without pasties would be like.

"Never," Katie admitted.

"And now that you've had one, do you like it?"

"Oh, yes." She grinned at him shyly. "Lots better than I'd like star-gazzy pie, I'm sure."

Mrs. Trelawny chuckled, and Ed and Lillian poked each other and snickered. Apparently the whole family had been in on the joke. Baby Patty, in a highchair between her mother and Gram, laughed out loud and beat the metal tray with her spoon.

"Put catsup on your pasty," Lillian mumbled and turned red at her own boldness. "That makes it even better."

"The thing about a pasty," Mrs. Trelawny said, "is it's a whole meal in one dish. Meat and taters and all tucked up in a pocket of crust. The miners used to carry them in their lunch buckets when they went underground. That and a cup of tea was a feast, you see."

"Pasties was better in Old Country," Gram said suddenly. "These are good enough, but in Old Country—"

"Everything was better there, wasn't it, Gram?" Mrs.

Trelawny's feelings weren't hurt at all.

"Most things," Gram agreed. "Not everythin'. Got refrigerators now—don't 'ave to worry about piskies turnin' the milk sour or spoilin' the puddin'."

Katie looked at Joan.

"Piskies are like elves, or Irish leprechauns, only they're Cornish," Joan explained.

Gram pointed a finger at Katie. "You 'eard the knackers again?" she demanded. "It's gettin' on the very date when the accident 'appened down there in the mine. July sixteenth it was, thirty years back. A sad day, a miserable day for Frank Pendarra and all of Newquay."

Mrs. Trelawny put out a warning hand. "Gram, please, no talk about knackers. You promised. It's wicked to pretend poor old Frank's son has become some evil little creature livin' on down there in the mine."

"Ain't pretendin'. I tell ye—"

"Well, don't." Mrs. Trelawny spoke with a firmness that cut off further talk. "Let Katie finish her pasty in peace. And guess what. We're havin' scalded cream for dessert."

Gram's scowl vanished. "With strawberries?"

"All the strawberries you want."

Scalded cream turned out to be another Cornish delicacy, made by the patient heating and skimming of whole milk. Heaped on top of rich red berries, it was delicious. Katie ate until she couldn't swallow another bite.

"Some of us poor souls have to work in the hot sun all afternoon," Mr. Trelawny said, roughing Ed's curly hair. "And some of us get to do just what they want to do. Which are you, mister?"

"Gonna play softball," Ed said, ducking out from under the tousling.

"I'm goin' to town with Ma," Lillian announced.

"And Joan is goin' to show Katie the caves," Mrs. Trelawny said. "That's something she ought to know about."

"Caves?" Katie was doubtful. The thought of going underground made her uncomfortable.

"Not real caves," Joan assured her. "They're places near the mine where the ground has sunk and made deep pits."

"It's something that happens over a long, long time," Mrs. Trelawny said. "The ground moves, you see, from all the diggin' and tunnelin', and after a while it just gives way." She looked at Katie with her serene smile. "It could still be happenin', that's what we think, Mr. Trelawny and I. Even though the minin' stopped thirty years ago, this hillside is honeycombed with tunnels. It's natural that there's still some settlin' and shiftin' goin' on."

Katie realized that this talk about the caves had a purpose behind it. "You mean that's what I heard the first night I was in Newquay?"

"Maybe so," Mrs. Trelawny said. "What I really mean is, our old Newquay ain't any more haunted than anyplace else."

" 'Tis so," said Gram. "Wait and see."

Katie wondered if Joan had told her parents what had

happened at the shaft house. Probably she had. And they didn't believe in the girl with golden hair any more than Joan did.

"Now you be sure to stop back here before you go home, Katie," Mrs. Trelawny said as the girls got ready for their walk. "I have some extra pasties for you to take to your folks." She gave Katie a hug and then pushed both girls toward the door. "We'll make a Cornish Cousin Jinny of you yet," she called after them.

"You have a terrific family," Katie said as they trudged along. "And your mom's a great cook." At the top of the hill, she threw her arms wide to the wind blowing across the meadow and took a deep breath. She loved the Trelawnys and felt much better for having spent time with them.

The good feeling lasted all afternoon, while they climbed around the caves that were really just deep, grassy ravines. It was twilight when Katie headed back to Uncle Frank's house, carrying a tray of pasties covered with foil.

Her mother was waiting on the front porch, lips pressed tight with anger.

"Jay's gone," she said before Katie could say a word. "He left right after you did this morning. And I tell you this," she added, her voice trembling with a whole day's worth of bottled-up rage, "if he gets into trouble again, I hope that sheriff arrests him. I've had absolutely all I can take!"

Chapter Eleven

"But we didn't do anything! We just went for a ride."

"You were grounded. You left when I wasn't looking. I'd call that doing something!"

Katie crouched on the stairs and listened to the furious voices on the front porch. She'd heard this kind of exchange many times in Milwaukee, but she couldn't make herself leave and go up to bed. It would be like leaving the scene of an accident that was about to happen. Someday Jay and her mother would go too far, say too much. Her family would be smashed to pieces.

"Well, you are grounded for three more days. And if I find out you got into more trouble today, you can plan to stay at home all summer. Is that clear?"

"There wasn't any trouble!"

The screen door slammed, and Jay stomped past the staircase on his way to the kitchen.

Katie tiptoed up to her room. After a few minutes she heard Jay and her mother come up, and soon the house was quiet. Still, she couldn't sleep. She kept thinking about the girl in the mirror. Who was she? What did she want? Maybe the sad white face was there in the glass right now. . . .

Gradually Katie became aware of a peculiar heaviness in the air. She curled into a tight ball and closed her eyes, the way she had long ago when she'd imagined monsters under her bed. She pulled the sheet over her head. And the tension grew. Something was terribly wrong. She stretched her aching muscles and got up, found the flashlight, and went out into the hall.

The mirror held nothing but the circle of the flashlight beam and her own dim reflection above it. *Go back to bed, silly*. It was what she wanted to do, but she couldn't. She felt as if someone—or something—were pushing her in the other direction. Like a ghost herself, she tiptoed down the stairs and drifted from room to room with the light dancing around her.

When she reached the kitchen, an overwhelming sense of danger pressed in upon her. Her hands shook, and the beam of light fluttered from one side of the room to the other. The table, the open windows, the refrigerator. The jar of peanut butter on the edge of the sink where Jay had left it. The tall cupboard. Just as her light settled on the cupboard, one of the doors swung open. Dishes rattled faintly, as if an invisible hand had touched them. Katie choked back a scream. Then, without asking herself why she did it, she dropped to her knees and pressed her ear to the worn linoleum.

It was there. First the groan that seemed to travel up through her fingers. Then the tremor. The peanut butter jar danced briefly on the sink and was still. The crickets' song stopped and began again. Katie rocked back on her heels and waited for her heart to stop its panicky thumping.

When she could move again, she snatched up the flashlight and ran through the house. The staircase loomed, a steep and treacherous hill that tripped her twice before she reached the top. She flew down the hall and threw open her mother's door.

"Katie! Good grief, you startled me!" Mrs. Blaine reached for the bedside lamp and switched it on as Katie collapsed on the foot of the bed. "You're white as a sheet—did you have a nightmare?"

Katie shook her head. "I have to tell you something," she whispered. "You probably won't believe me but—"

"Try me. I can't sleep, anyway."

In a rush of words, Katie poured out the story of the tremor she'd felt in the backyard the first night they'd been in Newquay, and the second tremor tonight. She told about the caves she and Joan had explored on the other side of the meadow, and Mrs. Trelawny's theory that the whole hill was settling. Instinct warned her not to mention the knackers, but she couldn't keep panic out of her voice. "Something's happening to this house, Mom," she finished. "It's like it's being attacked or something."

Mrs. Blaine listened patiently. "Old houses creak and settle all the time," she said when Katie stopped for breath. "And Mrs. Trelawny's probably right about the mine causing changes in the land surface. But surely changes like that take years, Katie. It's nothing to get so excited about."

"Yes, it is," Katie insisted. "We're in danger in this house, Mom. I can feel it."

"You what?"

"I have this feeling . . ." Katie read her mother's expression and hesitated.

"Now, Katie, don't!" her mother whispered. "You frighten me when you talk like that. *Little* children can't tell the difference between what's real and what they make up, but a girl your age should know. You're creating a problem when there's nothing to worry about."

Katie sighed. What was the use of explaining? "I'd better go to bed," she said. "Just forget it."

Her mother reached out and touched her hand. "You do that," she said in a gentler tone. "I don't mean to scold, dear heart, but I can't cope with make-believe problems when I have more real ones than I can handle. Do you understand?"

"Sure. Good night, Mom."

"Good night, dear. And Katie—not a word of this nonsense to Uncle Frank, hear?"

"Sure."

Back in her bedroom, Katie stood for a while at the window. She felt more alone than she'd ever been in her life. More alone than in the days before Tom Blaine, when her mother worked every day and Katie came home to an empty house. More alone than that first week at scout camp when she was the only one without a best friend. More alone than on that barely remembered night long ago when she'd stayed in the hospital to have her tonsils out. This was a different kind of loneliness. No one else would believe that there was danger threatening this house—danger from the shifting and sinking of the old mine, if you listened to Mrs. Trelawny, or from knackers, if you listened to Gram. No one believed except—the realization came suddenly—except the ghost-girl in the mirror. That must be what the girl was trying to say! Katie was certain of it.

The girl wanted to warn the Blaines and Uncle Frank. And no one but Katie was willing to listen.

For the next few nights, Katie forced herself to stay awake for an hour after the others had gone to bed. When all was still, she tiptoed into the hall and looked into the mirror for long, nerve-wracking minutes. But the ghost-girl didn't return, nor did Katie feel again the threat of danger that had sent her downstairs to explore.

"Where's your brother these days?" Joan asked one afternoon as they headed down the hill to visit Newquay's tiny library. "Haven't seen him at Skip's house for a while."

"He's still grounded," Katie explained. "He's been patching screens and fixing a broken step on the back porch. Most of the time he stays in his room."

"I bet he hates it."

"He doesn't talk to us," Katie admitted. "He just glumps around and glares."

"Still," Joan said, "it's a good thing he's stayin' home. The sheriff was at Poldeens' again yesterday."

"What for?" Katie felt familiar quivers in the pit of her stomach.

"Ed says somebody broke windows at the high school and splashed paint on the bricks. And there was another break-in at a summer cottage. The neighbors heard a motorcycle, so of course they thought of Skip. There's plenty of motorcycles around Newquay, but people always think of Skip." She smiled unexpectedly, a teasing grin. "Gram says it isn't Skip at all, it's the knackers. She says they're finding a way up from the mine—right through the shaft, maybe—and they're making mischief. She thinks they come up every night. . . ."

"What do knackers look like?" Katie asked. She didn't want to think about Skip Poldeen.

"Well, now," Joan began, imitating her grandmother's accent, "about three feet 'igh, they are, with big 'eads, squintin' eyes, a mouth that stretches from one ear to t'other. They can change shape, and if you get too close to 'em, they whisk clean away in a bit of smoke. . . . Hey, I have an idea!" The accent was forgotten. "Three days from now is the sixteenth—that's the anniversary of the accident. Let's go back to the shaft house and see what we can see."

Katie snorted. "You don't believe in knackers."

"But you do."

"I do not."

"Let's go anyway. Before the anniversary. Tomorrow night. I dare you, Katie."

Katie laughed nervously. "Okay," she agreed. "But not at night—my mom would have a fit. We'll go late in the afternoon. Is it okay if I ask Jay to come along?"

"He won't want to," Joan said. "Besides, I thought he was grounded."

"Today's the last day. I was thinking it would be a good idea if he came with us instead of—"

"Instead of running back to old Skip," Joan finished. "It's okay with me."

But, as Joan had predicted, Jay wasn't interested in a visit to the shaft house. "I've got other plans," he told her.

"Like what?"

"Nobody else's business."

"Joan says the sheriff was at Skip Poldeen's house again." Katie tried to say it casually.

"So what? Skip says Hesbruck blames him, whatever goes wrong. He hates motorcycles, that's all."

"But Skip's been in trouble before—"

"Look, Katie," Jay interrupted, "you mean well, but you've got Skip all wrong. He's not a bad guy—and he's *here*. I need a friend in this place—no one seems to understand that!"

Katie's face burned. For the hundredth time, she re-
solved to stop caring. Let Jay go his own unhappy way!

For the rest of the day she ignored him and concentrated
on dusting the books in the library. It was a lonely time,
except for an unexpected visit from Uncle Frank late in
the afternoon.

"Looks nice 'ere," he said. "Your ma's a good worker.
You're fair-to-middlin', too."

Katie smiled, hiding her surprise. "I don't mind dusting
books," she said. "The trouble is, I spend more time
reading than dusting."

Uncle Frank pulled out a book and put it back again.
He had something on his mind. "That boy, now," he said.
"'E's not such a bad 'un either. Thought 'e was at first.
Saucy enough, I'm sure. But I been watchin' 'im, and I
see that 'e's like me—like I was a long time ago. 'E's
lost 'is pa, and 'e can't get over it. I lost me family, and
I acted the same way. I was all alone, and I was scared.
It's a wicked feelin'—mad at the world, like, an' lookin'
for someone to thump."

Katie felt her eyes fill with tears. This was the longest—and friendliest—speech Uncle Frank had made since
the day they'd come to stay with him. Long after he'd
tottered off to his chair on the front porch, she was still
turning over his words in her mind.

Poor Jay—feeling alone and scared—mad at the world
and looking for someone to thump. In spite of herself,
she felt sorry for her stepbrother again.

"He's *not* such a bad 'un," she whispered to herself. "Uncle Frank is right. And Uncle Frank's a good 'un, too. Just like a real uncle." She smiled at the thought and ran the feather duster briskly across a whole row of bindings.

Chapter Twelve

"Jay didn't want to go with us, huh?" Joan sat on the curb in front of her house, long legs extended, head thrown back. She looked the way she had that first day when Katie and Jay wandered down the hill, except that now her smile carried a welcome. "I told you he wouldn't."

"He's swimming at Tuesday Lake," Katie explained, dropping down beside her. "I said he could still go along if he got back by four o'clock, but—" She glanced at the Poldeens' house and asked casually, "Is Skip around?"

"He's been gone all day, too."

Katie sighed. Jay had announced at breakfast that he was going to hike out to the lake and would take sandwiches and a thermos along. He'd been so open about his plans that Mrs. Blaine hadn't asked questions, though she looked as if she was biting her tongue. When he dropped a paperback and his tape player into the knapsack with his lunch, however, she'd seemed reassured. She'd even called, "Have a good time," when he clattered downstairs and out the front door soon after breakfast.

"I *hope* he's going alone," Mrs. Blaine said as she started to gather up the dishes. Katie was silent, and Uncle Frank had muttered, "That Poldeen is a bad 'un," putting all their thoughts into words.

Still, just because Skip was away from home didn't mean he and Jay were together. Katie turned away from the Poldeen house and concentrated on the afternoon's adventure. "Every time we go to the shaft house it rains," she said. "Look at that sky."

"Good weather for ghost-hunting," Joan agreed. "Or knacker-trapping," she added, rolling her eyes. "Come on inside a minute. I have to tell my ma we're ready to go."

They found Mrs. Trelawny in front of the television set, a heap of unmatched socks on the sofa beside her. She greeted Katie without her usual smile. "I've told Joan and now I'm tellin' you," she said. "I don't want you girls goin' inside that old shaft house again. Joan let it slip you went in there a while back, and I don't like it a bit."

"Ma, every kid in Newquay's been in there some time or other," Joan said, pouting. "It isn't dangerous."

"You heard me, missy."

"But how are we going to see ghosts or knackers if we don't go inside—"

"Ghosts! Knackers! I'm sick of hearin' about 'em. If

you like ghosts so much, listen to your gram's tales. You'll hear more about ghosts and knackers right here in your own house than you'll learn in that rickety old shaft house."

"We're just going to look around, Mrs. Trelawny," Katie said. "It doesn't mean anything."

"Katie saw a ghost the last time we were at the shaft house," Joan teased. "Didn't you, Katie? A girl with long blond hair and a pale face."

Katie nodded reluctantly. "I really did see her. She had beautiful golden hair, and when she walked she sort of limped."

"Oh, Katie! You're gettin' as bad as Gram."

"Gram ain't so bad," said a pert voice. The old lady peered at them from the doorway. "That's May Nichols you're talkin' of, missy, come back to warn of the danger. I ain't a bit surprised to hear it."

"Who's May Nichols?" Katie ignored Mrs. Trelawny's tight-lipped expression. If Gram knew something about the ghost-girl, Katie wanted to hear it.

"You ask old Frank an' he'll tell you," Gram said. She settled herself in an armchair. "Thirty years ago May Nichols was goin' to marry Frank's boy Kenny. Lovely girl, she was. Treated Frank like he was her own father."

"What happened to her?" Joan asked.

"When word came of the mine accident, she went to the shaft house to wait for news, same as 'undreds of others," Gram said. "Stayed there all night and the next day, too. They couldn't get 'er to leave, even after the rescue teams gave up. It was Frank finally made 'er go—

told 'er 'e needed a daughter to look after 'im, now that 'is son was gone. But it was too late by then. Caught the pneumonia, she did, waitin' and waitin'. Not three weeks after Frank lost 'is boy, 'e lost 'is May as well."

"Was she lame, Gram?"

"That she was. Broke 'er leg when she was a little mite, an' it never did 'eal right. No matter. She were a beauty."

Joan smacked her hands over her head. "You really did see a ghost then, Katie!" she exclaimed. "Now what do you say, Ma?"

"I say keep out of that shaft house. I say be home in time for supper. And that's all I say." Mrs. Trelawny scooped up the socks and marched out of the room.

"She doesn't want to talk about it 'cause she can't explain it," Joan whispered. "Come on, Katie, let's see if we can find poor May again. This is exciting! 'Bye, Gram."

The old lady caught Katie's wrist as the girls headed for the door. "If May Nichols's come back, it's because of them knackers," she warned. "She knows the danger same as I do. You listen to what she tells you."

"I will," Katie promised. *If only I could make other people listen, too,* she thought.

"How are we going to see a ghost if we can't go inside?" Joan grumbled as they walked across the meadows toward the slag heaps. Now that Gram had told them about May Nichols, Joan was a serious ghost-hunter. She'd chattered excitedly all the way up the hill.

"We'll have to climb up to the window and look in, that's all."

Joan pointed at the thickening clouds. "It was raining when you saw her before, and now it's going to rain again. Maybe she only appears in storms."

Katie decided to share her secret. "I saw her one other time, too," she admitted. "I saw her in a mirror at Uncle Frank's house."

Joan was outraged. "Why didn't you tell me?"

"You would have laughed." When Joan couldn't deny it, Katie hurried on. "Everybody would laugh. Or say I was making it up. Or say I'm flaky. Oh, Joan, she looked so sad—and so worried. It was like she was trying to tell me an important, terrible secret. And I think I know what it is. Something's going to happen to Uncle Frank's house, and May knows it. She's come back to warn us."

Joan's freckled face was somber as they pressed into the rising wind. "It makes me feel kind of weird," she said. "I mean, if *your* ghost is real, then maybe Gram's stories are true, too. Maybe there really are knackers—"

"No!" Katie exclaimed. "May Nichols is nothing like a knacker. She's good and she's beautiful. I think knackers are just something people dreamed up a long time ago to scare each other. Like Halloween spooks. May was a real person, and she's come back to help us, not to make trouble."

Joan looked as if she might argue the point, but just then lightning stitched a blue line across the clouds, and thunder rumbled close by.

"Let's run," Katie suggested. "We're going to get soaked."

They hurried across the yard that fronted the mine buildings and darted around to the back of the shaft house.

"We'll need two crates this time," Joan decided. "We can pile them under the window and look in together." She whirled on one toe like a ballerina and dropped to a crouch. "Here's the one we used last time. Let's push it up against the wall and then get a narrow one to go on top of it. Like steps."

The big crate was quickly moved into position, but they hunted in vain for a smaller box. Finally Joan led the way to a long, shedlike building she called the blacksmith shop. Behind it was a tumble of rotting railroad ties.

"The old tracks are over there." She pointed. "That's how they used to carry away the iron ore. I guess these ties were kept here for repairs. We can take a couple of them and stack 'em up. . . ."

It was heavy work, and the girls were soon hot and sticky in spite of the wind that was bringing the storm closer every minute. At last they maneuvered two ties into position, and Joan stepped back to admire their work.

"You can go first, Katie," she offered. "It's your ghost."

Katie scrambled up on the crate and then, less confidently, onto the ancient ties. She pushed open the window.

"See anything?" Joan scrambled up next to her, causing the wooden platform to tremble.

"Not yet."

Both girls leaned through the opening. "It's almost too dark to see," Katie whispered. She shivered as the dank breath of the mine filled her nostrils.

"Something's different in here," Joan said. "What is it?"

Katie caught her breath. "The ore car!" she exclaimed. "It was in the center of the room when we were here before. Now it's closer to the gate across the shaft. As if—"

"As if it's waiting to pick something up." Joan giggled nervously. "Or someone. Just like Gram said. Those old knackers are coming out of the shaft at night and running around Newquay making trouble—"

"Stop it!" Katie ordered. "Let's be quiet and wait. And keep looking over in that corner next to the shaft. That's where I saw May Nichols before."

For long minutes the girls hung, silent, on their teetering perch. The rain began to fall, gently at first and then harder. Drops ran down Katie's legs and into her sneakers.

"Do you see *any*thing?" Joan whispered. "My left foot's falling asleep and my neck's getting stiff."

Katie strained her eyes to pierce the shadows in the far corner. "I don't think she's here. Oh, I wish—" She stopped to listen. "Did you hear something then?"

"Rain on the roof."

"Not the rain," Katie said. "It was a voice! Listen!"

"Help us! Save us! Get us out of here!" The girls clutched each other as one strangled cry after another rang through the shaft house. The anguished shrieks rat-

tled against the walls.

"The ore car!" Katie gasped. "Look at it!"

The car had jolted into motion. It rolled a few feet and clanged heavily against the gate across the shaft.

"It's the knackers for sure! Oh, Katie, they *are* coming! Just like Gram said!" Joan leaped to the ground as the desperate cries from the shaft house were drowned by a mighty crack of thunder.

"Wait for me!" Katie screamed. She crouched and half jumped, half fell, turning her ankle as she landed. "I can't walk," she wailed. "What'll I do?"

The rain was sharp enough to sting bare arms and legs. "Hang on to my arm and hop!" Joan shouted. "Come on, Katie! I want to get away from here!"

Around the shaft house they hobbled, splashing through newly formed puddles and looking over their shoulders at every other step.

"We'd better go to my house," Katie panted. "I can't hop all the way down the hill."

"And I don't want my ma to see you," Joan said. "She'd just say 'I told you so.' And she'd *never* believe we heard the knackers."

In the shelter of the woods, Katie moved her ankle cautiously and discovered the pain was less severe than it had been.

"I guess it isn't broken." She looked at Joan, who was biting her lip. "Are you okay?"

"I guess so." Joan's face was chalky under its sprinkling of freckles, and she seemed close to tears. "Oh, Katie, I was so scared!"

"Me, too." But now that they'd left the mine behind them, Katie realized Joan's fear was more intense than her own. *Maybe it's because I've actually seen a ghost,* she thought. *Or maybe she's remembering all the scary stories Gram ever told her.*

"Let's keep going," Katie said. "You can call home from our house, and maybe Ed will come to meet you."

Uncle Frank was watching from the front porch as the girls made their slow way across the yard. He opened the screen door when they came up the steps and moved back to let them in.

"'Ere's two drowned rats," he announced. "Never saw a worse-lookin' pair."

Mrs. Blaine was in the kitchen. After a first flurry of concern about Katie's ankle, she grinned at Uncle Frank and nodded agreement. "You've described them perfectly, Uncle Frank. We ought to wring them out and hang them up to dry." She spilled chipped ice into a plastic bag and gave it to Katie to hold against the swelling. "That certainly looks sore."

"It is."

"Two drowned rats," Uncle Frank repeated. "You'll catch your death if you ain't careful."

Katie shuddered as trickles of water raced down her back. She kicked off her soggy shoes.

"Where did you go, anyway?" Mrs. Blaine asked. "You're as grubby as you are wet."

Katie kept busy with the icebag. "Just around. I fell down."

"But how did it happen? Did you stumble over something?"

Joan backed toward the door. "I better go home now," she said. "My ma's going to wonder where I am."

"Don't you want to call Ed?" Katie asked.

Joan shook her head. Clearly she'd rather face the walk alone than answer any of Mrs. Blaine's questions. "No problem. I'll run all the way."

Katie waved, and Mrs. Blaine went to the front door to watch Joan out of sight.

"You two been up to somethin'?" Uncle Frank asked. He looked disappointed when Katie said no. She hoped he wasn't going to start questions, too.

The thing to remember was that there was no such thing as a knacker. There just couldn't be. But those voices had come from the shaft; Katie was almost sure of it. If they weren't the voices of knackers, whose were they?

After twenty minutes with the ice pack, Mrs. Blaine helped Katie up the stairs and into bed. Soon afterward Katie heard Jay come home. She'd finished her tray of hamburger patty, mashed potatoes, peas, and milk, when he came upstairs and stopped at her partly opened door.

"You okay?" He sounded gruff, but Katie was pleased that he'd bothered to ask.

"I'm all right," she said. "I fell down, and my ankle puffed up, but it looks pretty good now. Did you have fun at the lake?"

"Fair. The water's too warm for swimming, and there's

lots of green stuff on the surface."

"Ugh."

He went on to his bedroom, and the house was still. For the first time Katie found herself missing a television set; she longed for something to distract her from thinking about the afternoon. There had to be an explanation for the voices—a believable one—but she couldn't find it. *I'll never believe in knackers*, she told herself. *Not unless I see one as clearly as I saw May Nichols*.

Moonlight streamed through the open windows, and the crickets began their nightly song as Katie burrowed deeper into her pillows. She didn't want to go to sleep. She'd probably dream about knackers pouring out of the mine shaft, with the ghost of May Nichols trying to hold them back. Or they might burst through the kitchen floor. . . .

Stop thinking, she ordered herself. But she knew she'd go on imagining terrible things until . . . until she went back to the shaft house to find out what was going on.

Chapter Thirteen

"I feel a lot better." Katie showed her mother how well she could walk. There was a little stiffness, but the swelling had disappeared overnight. The ankle was definitely strong enough to carry her to the mine.

"Do you need help today?" Katie almost wished her mother would say yes, but Mrs. Blaine shook her head.

"No, thanks. Uncle Frank asked me to sort through some old trunks in the attic, and I think I'll tackle that this morning."

"Then I'm going out for a while. To pick some wild-flowers."

It wasn't a real lie. The meadows were full of daisies and Queen Anne's lace, and Katie would remember to gather some on the way back from the shaft house.

"What about you, Jay?" Mrs. Blaine asked. "I could

use help pulling the trunks out to the center of the attic where I can get at them."

"I can help—for a while at least."

"Good. Uncle Frank mentioned that there's a stamp collection up there. He said if you want it, it's yours. He said it isn't particularly valuable, but it's a good collection to build on."

"He did?" Jay looked pleased.

Mrs. Blaine grinned. "Well, what he actually said was, 'It'll give the young feller somethin' safe to do. Can't break 'is neck ridin' up and down 'ills on a stamp collection.'"

Jay laughed in spite of himself, and Katie and her mother exchanged a quick glance.

It's wonderful to see them having fun together, Katie thought. *Maybe Jay's beginning to believe we need him in this family—and not just to move trunks in the attic. Maybe he's beginning to see that we really love him. . . .*

The meadow was at its liveliest, spangled with color and dancing in the wind. The mine buildings looked sleepy in the sun, and not at all scary. A yellow butterfly darted in front of Katie as she crossed the mine yard and went around to the back of the shaft house.

The crate and the railroad ties were under the window where she and Joan had left them. She wished Joan was with her now, but since Mrs. Trelawny had forbade Joan to go inside the shaft house, Katie hadn't invited her along. Katie climbed onto the crate with care, knowing that if she fell this time there would be no one to help her. When she stood up on the ties and leaned through the window, she realized she was trembling.

The shaft house was lighter than it had been yesterday. The ore car rested against the gate. Katie studied the shadowy corner beyond the shaft, but there was no sign of May Nichols's white face and shining hair.

Might as well get it over with. Gritting her teeth, Katie swung her legs over the windowsill and dropped to the crate on the other side. Her ankle twinged. Cautiously she stepped down to the floor.

The cool damp of the big room wrapped itself around her. There were small scratchings behind the boxes and scrap iron that lined the walls, and when she stopped to listen she heard the sound the wind made as it moved the machinery at the top of the shaft. On tiptoe, she crossed to the ore car.

There could be something—or someone—inside it. She fought a wave of panic. If knackers existed, one could be waiting there for some silly girl to come here all by herself. He could leap up and grab her—

She looked into the car and felt better. It was empty. No, not quite empty. Something lay at the bottom—a small boxlike object.

It was a tape player.

Katie blinked, half expecting the object to vanish. Then she climbed into the car and crouched on the bottom. The tape player was real. It was, in fact, one that she'd seen many times before.

She pressed the PLAY button, and the sound of whirring tape whispered from the machine. She switched to RE-

WIND, then started the tape again.

"Help us! Save us! Get us out of here!"

Katie shuddered and stopped the tape. The cries were terrifying even now, when she knew it wasn't knackers shrieking from the bottom of the shaft. She snatched up the player and scrambled from the car.

Tears of rage blurred her eyes as she scrambled up on the crate and struggled through the open window. The ties teetered underfoot, and she forced herself to move more slowly. But when she was safely on the ground again, she began to run, the sore ankle forgotten.

"I hate him! I *hate* him! And he's going to be sorry!" She tore around the side of the shaft house just as Jay appeared at the other end of the building.

They stared at each other.

"I hate you!" Katie screamed. "You're just—just gross! I s'pose you came back for this." She lifted the tape player over her head and threw it with all her might.

"Hey!" Jay lunged forward, but Katie reached the spot where it had fallen first and stood over it, her fists clenched.

"I hope it's wrecked!" she roared. "Then you can't use it again to play mean, nasty tricks on people. I bet you thought it was really funny when I darned near broke my ankle!"

Jay stepped back. "It was just a joke," he protested. "Where's your sense of humor? You said you were going to hunt for knackers or whatever you call 'em, and we just thought—"

"We!" Katie cringed. It was even worse than she'd thought. "You and—and that awful Poldeen! That big nothing was there laughing at us, too. Oh, I think you're the meanest, low-downest—you know what?" She felt as if she might explode into a million tiny pieces. "I actually wanted you for my brother, Jay Blaine. I thought you were neat. Well, that was the dumbest idea I ever had. You can go back to Milwaukee tomorrow, as far as I'm concerned. I hope you do. I hope I never see you again!"

She kicked the tape player out of her way and stalked past him. She'd surprised herself with the depth of her anger. It was as if all the harsh words she'd been holding back for months had come flying out when she pictured Jay and Skip Poldeen laughing at her and Joan.

She whirled suddenly and faced Jay, who had been following at a safe distance. "Where were you yesterday, anyway?" she demanded. "You couldn't have climbed into the cage! Even you wouldn't have been dumb enough to do that."

"I was hiding on the other side of the ore car," Jay muttered.

"And that whole story about going to Tuesday Lake was a lie?"

"No, it wasn't. I hiked out there in the morning, but the swimming was no good so I came back early. I ran into Skip, and we sat around shooting the breeze for a while. I told him you and Joan were going to the shaft house to look for knackers, and he said we ought to go there, too. He doesn't like Joan—she puts him down all the time." Jay paused. "The tape was my idea, not his."

Katie walked on. "I wouldn't be proud of *that*."

"I'm not. But I didn't mean to scare you that much. I thought you'd guess it was a joke."

Katie wondered if he was as sorry as he sounded. She hoped so.

"I even thought maybe you'd catch on right away and climb inside to look around. That's why I made the ore car move."

"You and your buddy Skip," Katie said bitterly.

"Skip was outside. He moved the crate away from the window after I climbed in, so you wouldn't know anyone else was there. He was hiding behind one of the other buildings. . . . What're you doing?"

They had reached the meadow, and Katie plunged off the path. "I'm picking wildflowers, obviously. I said I was going to pick 'em, and I'm doing it."

"So you told a sort of lie, too," Jay reminded her, but without his usual bite. "You didn't want your mother to know you were going to the shaft house—"

"Oh, be quiet!" She wished he'd go away. Instead he just stood in the tall grass watching her, the remains of the shattered tape player dangling from one hand.

"Katie, I want to tell you something. If you knew—"

"I know all I want to know," Katie snapped. "I don't want to hear about how Skip Poldeen is really a good kid and I don't have a sense of humor and nobody loves poor you. Just leave me alone!" She turned her back and snatched handfuls of daisies.

"It wasn't any of those things," Jay said. "But I'll leave

you alone, if that's what you want. Who cares, anyway?"

When she looked again, he was nearly to the road that led into the woods. His shoulders were hunched, and he walked fast, almost but not quite running.

I guess I told him! she thought with satisfaction. She turned back to the wildflowers and tugged at a stubborn stalk of Queen Anne's lace till it came out of the ground, roots and all.

Chapter Fourteen

"He's gone! He's been gone all night. His bed hasn't been slept in!" Mrs. Blaine's face was ashen. She stood in the doorway of Jay's room, staring at the unwrinkled bed. "He's never done *this* before. Oh, Katie, where in the world could he be?"

"I don't know."

"Did he say anything to you about running away? He was awfully quiet yesterday, wasn't he? Even more so than usual."

"He didn't say he was going to run away last night." *But I said plenty to him,* Katie thought as she turned away to hide her expression. Jay was probably on his way back to Milwaukee. She'd have to tell her mother he'd been threatening to go ever since they arrived in Newquay. And she'd have to tell her about yesterday's fight, too.

"Well, I'm going to call the sheriff." Mrs. Blaine started for the stairs. "And I'm going to call that Poldeen person, too. If they went off somewhere on the motorcycle and had an accident—"

Uncle Frank stood in the parlor arch waiting for them. "What's 'appened?" he demanded. "Somethin' wrong with the boy, is it?"

"He's been out all night." Katie realized her mother was crying and attempting to hide it. "Oh, Uncle Frank, I could kill him for scaring me like this—and yet if he's lying in a ditch somewhere, I'll never forgive myself. I honestly don't know how to handle him! I don't know what to do next."

"'Ere, now." The old man put his arms around Mrs. Blaine's shoulders. "You 'ave a good cup of tay before you do anythin' else, that's a good girl. Nothin' like a cup of tay to make a body feel better."

Suddenly he was in charge, drawing Mrs. Blaine down the hall past the telephone to the kitchen. Katie followed. It was the first time she'd seen her mother too upset to cope. She'd been strong even when Tom Blaine died, saving her tears for when she was alone.

"You 'eat the kettle, missy," Uncle Frank ordered. "And put some tay in the pot."

Katie obeyed while Uncle Frank pressed Mrs. Blaine into a chair. He patted her arm and offered her a wadded handkerchief from his sweater pocket. When the water was boiling, Katie brought the teapot to the table and found cups on the shelf.

"That's better," Uncle Frank said. "Drink up now."

"I should be calling the sheriff."

"In a bit. You drink your tay first."

Katie collapsed into a chair. After a moment Uncle Frank sat down, too, and took a noisy sip of tea.

"I have this terrible feeling," Mrs. Blaine quavered. "I can see Jay hurt—"

"No, you can't," Uncle Frank said. "Up to some devilment, I don't doubt, but that don't mean 'e's been 'urt."

Katie's mother leaned back and brushed a hand across her eyes. "I am just so tired," she murmured. "I feel as if I've been fighting with him for years, and losing the battle. Maybe I've lost it already. I mean, maybe I've lost *him*. The thing is, he isn't a bad boy"—she looked at Uncle Frank, wanting him to understand—"I know that, even when he drives me crazy. He needs someone more patient than I am, someone who knows more about boys. I get so mad, but it's only because I'm worried. I love him, for goodness' sake!"

"Maybe he took the bus back to Milwaukee," Katie suggested timidly.

"Oh, no!" Her mother was shocked. "Did he say—"

"I'm here."

They all jumped, and Uncle Frank's cup rocketed across the table, spilling a stream of tea on the oilcloth. Jay stood on the other side of the screen door. His face was pinched, and lumpy with mosquito bites. His straight blond hair was tousled. He opened the door and came in, his eyes on Mrs. Blaine, a stunned expression on his face. Katie wondered how long he'd been standing there.

"I just meant to go out for a little while last night," he

said. "Sorry about that."

Mrs. Blaine opened her mouth and closed it. "What happened to your jeans?" she asked, when she'd found her voice.

Jay looked down, as if puzzled by the question. "Oh, yeah," he mumbled. "I chopped 'em off. Too hot."

He started across the kitchen toward the hallway, and Mrs. Blaine jumped up. "We were worried to death!" she exclaimed. "I was sure you'd been in an accident."

"I said I was sorry." The reply was subdued. "I better clean up."

"Not till you tell me where you've been all night," Mrs. Blaine insisted. "I want to know."

"Can't." The single word was like a groan. Katie, her mother, and Uncle Frank stared after him as he left the kitchen. Mrs. Blaine sank back into her chair.

"Let it go for now," Uncle Frank said. He was pale, as if his effort to be reassuring had exhausted him. "I'm goin' for a nap," he said.

"Don't forget your pills," Mrs. Blaine said automatically, her eyes still on the doorway where Jay had disappeared. "I'm sorry we've loaded our troubles on you, Uncle Frank."

The old man made a dismissing gesture. He squinted down the hall. "Car comin' across the field," he said. His footsteps dragged as he went to his bedroom.

Even before she followed her mother to the door, Katie guessed who their visitor would be. Sheriff Hesbruck's tall frame loomed dark against the morning sun. He nodded a greeting as Mrs. Blaine let him in.

"Your stepson home?"

"Yes—what's wrong?"

Here it comes, Katie thought. The overwhelming relief she'd felt when Jay returned was dispelled. She heard again the words she'd hurled at him yesterday: *I actually wanted you for my brother, Jay Blaine. . . . That was the dumbest idea I ever had.* She'd told him she hated him, and last night he'd sneaked out and done something awful to prove he didn't care about her or anybody else.

"Want to talk to him about a fire over on the county line road," the sheriff said. "Happened about midnight."

"A fire!" Mrs. Blaine gasped. "Jay wouldn't—"

"I'm not saying he did anything, ma'am," the sheriff said gently. "But it sure enough was arson—an old abandoned barn burned right down to the foundations."

"But why do you want to talk to Jay?"

The sheriff shifted from one booted foot to the other. "Same story as last time I was here. Somebody on the county line road thinks they heard a motorcycle about the time the barn went up. I stopped at Poldeens'—Skip hasn't been home since yesterday afternoon. And your boy's a friend of Poldeen's."

"Was anybody hurt in the fire?" Katie asked.

The sheriff looked up the stairs, as if he knew Jay was there and possibly listening. "Doesn't make any difference," he said. "Happens nobody was hurt, but they could have been. Took the whole volunteer fire department to control the fire. And if it had gotten away from them, it could have burned thirty or more acres of crops. A summer's work for some good men. *They* would have been hurt plenty!" He moved toward the stairs. "I want to talk to your boy."

"I'll call him," Mrs. Blaine said in a low voice.

Katie felt as if she were suffocating, caught between the sheriff's accusing words and her mother's panic. Arson was a real crime—far more serious than breaking into a cottage and taking a can of beans. If Jay was guilty, he could go to jail! Katie slipped around the sheriff and went out on the front porch to think.

The sunlight and bird song seemed out of place, like happy music at a funcral. Katie considered going down the hill to pour out her troubles to Joan, but she didn't really want to tell anyone what the sheriff suspected. Anyway, it could still all be a mistake. The sound of a motorcycle in the night didn't mean that Skip Poldeen and Jay had started the fire. But why had Jay looked and sounded so strange if he hadn't done anything wrong? And if he wasn't with Skip, where had he been all night? Katie went down the steps and along the road, her head throbbing with painful questions, until she found herself in the leafy tunnel that led through the woods.

Here in the shadows it was warmer, and the air was heavy with the scent of pine. Katie thought about Jay, and about poor, sad May Nichols, and about Uncle Frank's son, Kenny, and about Uncle Frank himself, who had once been as unhappy as Jay was now. She thought about the bus ride north to Newquay and how she'd dreamed happy dreams of life in Newquay. *What a baby I was!* She put her head down on her knees and sighed.

Gradually, she became aware of a pungent smell,

stronger than the pine fragrance, definitely disturbing. She followed the odor along the road, and when it became very strong she pushed her way through the underbrush. A dark blue bundle lay on the ground, partly hidden by a raspberry bush. It unrolled when she picked it up, and she found herself holding two long denim tubes. Blue-jean legs. The smell of gasoline filled her nostrils.

Katie froze, as if the denim scraps were snakes that might strike out at any moment. She heard the sheriff's car start up back at the house, and she held her breath as it came across the meadow and into the woods. She wanted to peek out to see if Jay was in the back seat, but she didn't dare. Long after the sound of the motor faded, she stood where she was, the heavy, sweetish fumes rising around her.

When at last she made her way back to the road, tears were running down her cheeks. At the turn in the road, she came face to face with Jay.

He stopped when he saw what she was holding. "I might have known it," he said, sounding lost. "Well, you can really get even this time, kid. Just call up the sheriff and tell him the great girl detective and spook-hunter has solved his case!"

Chapter Fifteen

Katie looked down at the gasoline-soaked denim she was holding. The smell was very strong. Her stomach felt queasy.

"Why would you set fire to a barn?" she asked. "Why would *anybody* do that?"

"I didn't!" Jay snapped. "You won't believe it now, but that's the truth. I didn't have anything to do with the fire."

"Then how—"

"I took a walk down to Poldeens' last night after the rest of you were in bed. Skip said he was going for a ride and I could come along if I wanted to. It was great! You don't know what it's like to ride a motorcycle. Nobody does, if they haven't tried it. You're out there between the road and the sky, and you smell the grass and feel the wind. . . ." He broke off, red-faced.

"So what happened?"

"We were just coasting along, and all of a sudden Skip turned onto a side road and pulled up in front of a barn. He took a can of gasoline out of the trunk on the back of the cycle, and he said we were going to have a bonfire. I thought he was kidding at first. Then I tried to stop him, but he told me to shut up. He said the barn was just an old wreck, but it had some hay stored in it and it would make a terrific fire. I tried to grab the can, and some of the gas splashed on my jeans. Skip lit a match"—Katie gasped—"and he said if I didn't back off I could be part of the bonfire, it was all the same to him." Jay's color faded as he repeated the ugly words. "I thought we were friends, but . . . anyway, I got out of there fast. I looked back once and saw the fire, and after that I cut across fields because I knew the fire department would be coming. When I got back here, I chopped off the jeans with my knife because the gas smell was so strong."

"You walked back?" Katie remembered the exhausted, insect-bitten face that had looked in at them through the screen door a couple of hours before. "How could you find your way in the dark?"

"I saw the shaft house at the top of the hill in the moonlight and just kept going." Jay shrugged. "So that's it, and you might as well call the sheriff. I don't expect you to believe me, even though it's true."

"I do believe you," Katie said. Jay had lied to her in the past, but she was certain he was telling the truth this time. "Mom'll believe you, too. When you weren't in your room this morning, she felt really bad. She told Uncle Frank you were a good person, and she told the sheriff—" Katie thought of the sheriff's cold eyes as he started toward the stairs to look for Jay. "What did *you* tell him?"

"That I didn't set the fire. That I'm not going to rat on anybody else, so it's no use asking me questions."

"Then what's going to happen?"

"Who knows? He's still looking for Skip."

They started back toward the house. "Aren't you really going to tell him about the jeans?" Jay asked. "I wouldn't blame you, I guess. After yesterday."

Katie rolled up the pieces of denim and threw them back into the woods. The last few hours had been so painful that she'd almost forgotten what had happened at the shaft house. "I guess I can take a joke," she said slowly. "Or I could if Skip Poldeen wasn't in on it."

"That's all it was—a joke. I mean, who believes in knackers—except old Mrs. Trelawny?"

"Not me," Katie retorted. "Not Joan either. We just went back to the shaft house for the fun of it, and be- cause—because—I don't believe in knackers, but I do believe in ghosts," she said defiantly. "I have reasons."

Jay scuffed his toes in the gravel and looked at Katie uneasily. "I saw her," he said.

"Saw who?"

"The girl with the yellow hair. The one you said was in the shaft house the first time you went there. I saw her day before yesterday, after you kids ran away. That's what I wanted to tell you yesterday."

Katie couldn't believe her ears. "You *saw* her?"

"In the corner next to the shaft. I was behind the ore car, and I balanced the tape recorder on the edge when I stood up. There was a noise behind me—sort of a sigh—and when I turned around, there she was."

"Did she say anything?"

Jay snorted. "Do you think I stood around making conversation? I went through that window faster than you did. The tape player fell into the car, and I never even noticed it was gone till I got home."

Suddenly Katie felt almost lighthearted. Jay had seen May Nichols! And he hadn't set the barn fire; he'd even tried to stop Skip Poldeen from starting it. The world wasn't quite as dismal as it had looked a few minutes ago.

Jay's next words cut sharply through her rising mood. "If I get out of this barn-burning mess, I'm leaving," he said. "I've got it all figured out. I can call that social worker I saw last winter, and I'm pretty sure he'll find a place for me to stay in Milwaukee. A foster home. It'll only be till I'm out of school, and then I'll be on my own."

"A foster home?" Katie repeated. "But you have a home."

"That's your home. Not mine. I was dumped on you and your mother, that's all. What do you need me around for?"

Katie struggled to keep her voice steady. "We're a family," she said. "We *are*, Jay. I know you heard what Mom was saying in the kitchen this morning. She loves you. She only gets mad because she's worried."

"Well, when I leave, she won't have to worry any-more." Jay kicked a stone and sent it skittering into the brush. Almost at once, a graceful brown shape moved out ahead of them. Liquid eyes studied them, and the white tail twitched. After a few seconds, a dappled fawn appeared and stood behind its mother.

Katie held her breath. "Oh, Jay, look," she whispered. "Isn't that the most beautiful thing you've ever seen?"

"Neat," Jay said, but he said it as if he was thinking about something else.

Katie bit her lip. Newquay had offered them its love-liest sight, and it wasn't enough. She had a strange, sad feeling that her stepbrother was already far away.

Once again, the old house seemed to be waiting for something. Katie remembered thinking that the first time she'd stepped inside the front door, and tonight the tension was greater than ever.

Jay had settled in the library with a science-fiction paperback he'd brought from home. Mrs. Blaine and Uncle Frank were on the front porch. Katie wandered from one room to another through air that was heavy with secrets. She stared long and hard into the mirror at the end of the upstairs hall, but May Nichols didn't appear. In the parlor and kitchen Katie knelt and put her ear to the floor, but heard nothing. Still, the feeling of im-pending danger persisted.

The telephone rang, and Mrs. Blaine hurried in from

the porch to answer it. Jay listened from the library door-way. *Maybe that's it,* Katie thought. *We're all expecting the sheriff to call or come back. It's us, not the house, that's waiting.* But the caller was Joan, suggesting a hike to Tuesday Lake the next day. When Katie hung up, the ominous stillness settled in once more.

At nine o'clock Uncle Frank came inside, his step firmer than usual as he marched down the hall. He passed Katie, who was working on a jigsaw puzzle at the dining room table, and went to the library door.

"Got somethin' to say to you, boy," he announced. "I 'ad a boy once, y'know."

"I know." Jay sounded startled; Uncle Frank seldom spoke to him directly.

"'E was a good boy, but not so lucky as you," the old man went on. "Died young, 'e did—thirty years ago tomorrow. You think of that, boy. You got lots to be glad for—most of all just bein' alive. You remember that when you feel like the world's goin' against you, 'ear?"

"Okay." Jay must have offered Uncle Frank the big leather chair. The old man shook his head and backed away. "'Ave to go to bed," he muttered. "Tired. Seems like I'm always tired. Wanted to tell you that, though. You're not a bad young feller. I like 'avin' a boy around again."

This time as Uncle Frank made his way back through the dining room, he laid a hand briefly on Katie's head. "Good night, missy."

"Good night, Uncle Frank."

Later, when the long evening had ended and Katie was in bed, she wished she'd jumped up right then and given Uncle Frank a hug. The wild-looking, frightened old man who'd shouted at her the day they arrived in Newquay had turned into a different person. The real Uncle Frank was kind and caring, not at all the way he'd seemed.

Died young, 'e did—thirty years ago tomorrow. . . . The anniversary of the mine accident had finally arrived, and tomorrow Gram Trelawny would be watching for knackers around every corner. Katie wondered if Joan had told her family about the voices in the shaft house. Probably not. Mrs. Trelawny would say Joan had imagined the whole thing, and Gram would be frightened out of her wits. *I'll have to tell Joan about Jay and the tape player tomorrow,* she decided. *When we go out to the lake. . . .*

Sleep was impossible. The old house creaked and groaned in a rising wind. The curtains danced at the windows, and the pages of a magazine lying on the dresser lifted and turned.

The bed moved.

For a second or two, Katie wasn't sure. Then she heard a crash, and a door opened in the hall. She snatched up her flashlight and ran out, nearly crashing into Jay.

"What the heck was that?" he demanded. "My lamp fell over. The whole darned house shook."

"Jay, look!" Katie pointed down the hall with the flashlight to where the mirror hung at a crazy angle. "There she is!"

From out of the darkness the golden-haired girl limped

into the beam of light. Her lips moved and her eyes were wide and frightened. One hand gestured frantically.

"She—she's saying something," Jay muttered. "But I can't—"

The hallway filled with wind. The girl's lips moved again, and now a thin, sweet whisper filled the hallway, like the voice of the wind itself.

"Go," it said. "Go now." And then, as Katie clutched Jay's arm, the vision faded, the wind stopped blowing, and the mirror crashed to the floor.

Chapter Sixteen

"Katie! Jay! What's going on out here?"

Mrs. Blaine stood silhouetted in her bedroom doorway. Katie threw herself into her mother's arms.

"Mom, something awful's happening! The house moved—"

"Oh, Katie, stop it!" Mrs. Blaine stepped back. "Stop screaming and tell me what this is all about."

"The house is—"

"Look at the mirror," Jay interrupted.

Mrs. Blaine stared at the shattered glass. "How in the world did that happen?" she demanded. "What's going on here? That mirror meant a great deal to Uncle Frank— he told me it was to have been a wedding present for his son. He's going to feel just terrible when he finds out—"

Katie and Jay exchanged a look. This was no time to

mention May Nichols's appearance in the mirror.

"Mom, the house shook just now," Katie repeated. "My bed moved, and Jay's lamp fell over. And then the mirror slipped off the wall. Didn't you feel *anything?*"

"No, I didn't," Mrs. Blaine snapped. "I was sleeping, and that's what you should have been doing, too. Come on, Katherine Jane, we don't need play-acting in the middle of the night."

"We have to get out of here," Jay said. "This old barn could fall down any minute."

"Now, you stop that!" Mrs. Blaine turned on her step-son. "Haven't you caused enough trouble and heartache for one day? I don't know what this is all about, and I don't want to. A mirror doesn't just jump off the wall—"

"What's 'appenin' up there? What's goin' on?" Uncle Frank was at the foot of the stairs.

In the half-light from the bedroom, Jay looked as if he'd been slapped. Katie went to the top of the stairwell on legs that threatened to fold under her. "We'll be right down," she called. "Just a minute, Uncle Frank."

"You aren't going anywhere except to bed," Mrs. Blaine said. "I'll explain to Uncle Frank that there's been an accident, though *how* I'll explain it I can't imagine."

"You can tell him the truth," Jay suggested in a voice so coldly adult that Mrs. Blaine paused. "This place is collapsing, no matter what you think. Stuff is falling off the walls. We have to get out."

For the first time Mrs. Blaine seemed less certain. She looked from Jay to Katie, then turned back to the broken mirror. "You mean neither of you touched the mirror?"

"No!" Katie exclaimed. "It fell by itself. And my bed moved, Mom. It really did. If you'd been awake, you'd have felt it, too."

Mrs. Blaine pursed her lips. "I suppose I can tell Frank the house is settling a little, and the mirror fell," she said slowly. "We can have someone come and check the foundations."

"It's too late for that," Jay said. "We have to leave."

"What's 'appenin'?" Uncle Frank was beginning to sound desperate. "Somebody come 'ere!"

With a sigh, Mrs. Blaine went down the stairs, leaving Katie and Jay in the shadowy hall.

"I don't know about you, but I'm leaving," Jay said. "You heard what that—that thing in the mirror said."

"She's not a thing," Katie protested. "Her name is— was—May Nichols. She was going to marry Uncle Frank's son, and when he was killed, she got sick and died, too. Joan's Gram told me."

"Well, I don't care what her name is," Jay retorted. He glanced over his shoulder as if he expected the spirit to reappear at any moment. "She meant it when she said 'Go,' and I'm taking her advice. If you're smart, you'll come, too."

Dazed, Katie let him pull her down the stairs. Angry words from the parlor stopped them at the front door.

"—Not so," Uncle Frank shouted. "There's nothin' wrong with my 'ouse. You've been listenin' to Nancy Trelawny an' 'er wailin' about them knackers."

Mrs. Blaine broke in with a soothing murmur.

"No! Nobody's goin' to poke around 'ere and tell me

my 'ouse is fallin' down. I won't 'ave it!"

Katie shook off Jay's hand and went into the parlor. Uncle Frank, in wrinkled pajamas, was sitting on the high-backed sofa. Mrs. Blaine was beside him. When Uncle Frank saw Katie, he smacked his knee with a gnarled fist. "You're the one, missy," he roared. "You're the one listens to Nancy and brings back tales—"

Katie realized that there was more than anger in Uncle Frank's eyes. There was fear, too.

"You felt the house move tonight, didn't you, Uncle Frank?" She asked it hurriedly, not daring to look at her mother.

"I never! There's nothin' wrong with this 'ouse, I tell ye!"

Katie sat down at Uncle Frank's other side. Jay watched and listened from the doorway.

"I don't believe in knackers, Uncle Frank," she said. "Honestly I don't. I know your son could never be changed into an evil spirit. I don't think Gram Trelawny believes that either. It's just a kind of game she plays. But there's something else. Uncle Frank, there *is* a ghost—I've seen her, and Jay has seen her, too. We saw her tonight."

Mrs. Blaine gasped. "Katie, be still this minute."

"She has long yellow hair," Katie continued. "And she limps when she walks. Tonight Jay and I both saw her in the mirror upstairs. She told us to get out of the house right away."

Uncle Frank fell backward against the cushions as if someone had pushed him. "May?" he whispered. "You seen my May?"

"Katie, this is unforgivable!" Mrs. Blaine exclaimed. "Go upstairs at once."

"What did my May tell you?"

"She told us to leave," Katie repeated. "Uncle Frank, the house is in danger, and May Nichols is trying to save us. She's trying to save us all, because she loves you so much. Mrs. Trelawny told me the ground above the mine has been shifting and sinking for a long time. I've heard it and felt it myself—once in the backyard, and once in the kitchen."

"Katie, *please*." Mrs. Blaine sounded totally exasperated.

Uncle Frank drew a long, shuddering breath. "May was like my own," he said. "Lost a son and then a daughter, I did, all in a month. And now you tell me she's come back. . . . If my May says go, you best go. I ain't leavin', but you go."

Mrs. Blaine jumped up. "This has gone far enough," she said. "Uncle Frank, I'll get you a nice cup of warm milk to calm you down, and then we'll all go back to bed. We've had enough talk about ghosts and mysterious warnings for one night."

"I did feel the 'ouse move," Uncle Frank admitted. "Felt it tonight and felt it lots of other times, I 'ave. But I'm not leavin'. This is my place."

"But you can't stay here," Katie protested. "Not if the house is going to collapse."

Uncle Frank stood up, looking dignified in spite of his pajamas and his ragged mane of hair. "I want you to go," he told Mrs. Blaine. "Go right now."

"But we can't leave you—"

"I asked you to come an' I'm askin' you to go. I don't want you 'ere anymore."

"Now look what you've done, Katie," Mrs. Blaine stormed. "This is all your fault."

The house shuddered. Mrs. Blaine sat down hard as a vase danced over the edge of an end table, and the painting above the sofa slipped sideways. Out in the foyer, the long-silent grandfather clock chimed twice.

"Let's move." Jay spoke from the doorway. "Talk it over outside if you want to."

Mrs. Blaine looked around the parlor unbelievingly. Her gaze settled on the fallen vase. "Maybe we'd better...." She hesitated, then made up her mind. "Jay and Katie are right, Uncle Frank, we'd better leave. We'll go down the hill for the rest of the night—I'm sure the Trelawnys will take us all in. And tomorrow we can get a builder to come up here and look—"

The house moved again.

Jay threw open the front door. Katie and her mother each took one of Uncle Frank's arms and tried to pull him to his feet, but he shook them off. "Go along!" he shouted. "Get out!"

Mrs. Blaine stepped back. "Katie, you and Jay go outside. Wait for us—Uncle Frank and I will be out in a few minutes."

"Go!" the old man bellowed, his face becoming dangerously red. "Go now. All of you!" He raised an arm as if he would drive them from the house.

Mrs. Blaine gave up and let Katie pull her toward the

door. "We're going to wait for you right outside," she called over her shoulder. "You know you can't stay here alone. . . ."

As soon as they were out on the porch, the door was slammed behind them. The key turned in the lock, and Uncle Frank looked out at them triumphantly through the glass.

"We shouldn't have given in to him," Mrs. Blaine cried. "He's so upset, he doesn't know what he's doing. He could have another heart attack and die in there!"

Jay pulled them down the steps and out onto the road. "You run for help," he ordered Katie. "I'll try to get him out."

"No, you won't!" Mrs. Blaine panicked. "You can't! Oh, this is crazy!"

Katie dashed away, hardly aware that she was barefoot and wearing nothing but one of Tom Blaine's extra-large T-shirts and the bottom half of her shortie pajamas. She hesitated only a moment at the woods, then plunged ahead, following the turns in the road from memory. At the other end, the gentle meadow wind seemed to speed her down the hill into the sleeping town. She flew past dark houses and empty fields until she recognized the Trelawnys' rooftop against the sky.

"Joan! Mrs. Trelawny!" She beat on the door, turned the knob and found it open. In the dark entryway she screamed again.

Mr. Trelawny, in T-shirt and shorts, was the first one down the stairs. Joan and her mother were right behind him, followed by Edward and Lillian. Mrs. Trelawny threw her arms around Katie.

"What is it, girl? What's happened?"

"The house—" Katie sobbed. "The house is moving—I think it's going to fall down—and Uncle Frank won't come out. He won't listen. . . ."

Mr. Trelawny dashed back up the stairs, returning almost at once in trousers and shoes. "I'm goin'," he shouted. "Don't know what's goin' on up there, but I'll find out."

Katie slipped from Mrs. Trelawny's embrace and ran after him.

"Wait for me," Joan cried.

Katie felt as if she were caught up in a nightmare and must run forever. Going uphill was harder; she was aware now of her scratched and bleeding feet. Lights flickered on in some of the houses, and she glimpsed Mr. Trelawny pounding ahead of her. Scared-looking faces peered from windows.

Katie was only a few steps behind Mr. Trelawny when they hurtled out of the woods. He stopped so suddenly that Katie bumped into him.

"What's this, now?" he exclaimed. "Look at that, will you?"

Katie stared. The old house loomed like a lighted ship in the darkness, a ship on the slope of a wave. The whole facade was tilted. Katie's mother stood out in front, alone on the road.

"Mom!" Katie screamed. "Where's Jay?"

Mrs. Blaine pointed at the house. "I—I couldn't stop him. He broke a window and went in!"

Mr. Trelawny took the porch steps two at a time and disappeared through the gaping parlor window. Katie clung to her mother as the ground trembled under their feet and the house groaned.

"I tried to hold on to him," Mrs. Blaine sobbed. "He broke away from me—oh, Katie, they'll be killed in there. I know it!"

The yard began to fill with people, most of them in bathrobes. Joan pressed close to Katie, and Mrs. Trelawny stood behind them, her face grim.

The house tilted more sharply.

"Is my husband in there?" Mrs. Trelawny's voice was steady.

Katie nodded. "And Jay and Uncle Frank."

"It'll be all right," Mrs. Trelawny said. "If the gas line just don't break."

As if the words were a signal, there was a dull explosion in the back of the house. The lights went out, and the house moved like a great dark animal settling on its haunches. Flames shot from the kitchen windows.

"She's finished now," a man's voice said. "Look at that!"

As the crowd surged to the side of the house, Katie saw Jay's face through the glass in the front door. The door opened partway, then stopped, jammed by the sloping porch floor. Katie ducked from her mother's grasp and darted toward the house and up the steps.

"Katie, no!"

The porch was split from end to end. The front section, attached to sturdy posts, remained level; the inner part sloped sharply. Katie grasped the doorknob and pulled, without hope.

Jay looked out at her, his face white and anguished. Where were Uncle Frank and Mr. Trelawny? She pulled again as Jay's shoulder thudded against the door. Then the porch shifted under her feet, and the two sections of the floor separated. Katie dropped, screaming, into the opening between them. She scrambled to her feet just as the door flew open overhead and Jay stumbled into the hole beside her. Behind him, Katie glimpsed Uncle Frank lying on the floor, and Mr. Trelawny crouched and coughing. Smoke billowed around them. At the end of the hallway, the kitchen door was a blazing rectangle.

"My arm," Jay gasped. He sagged against Katie, and she clutched at the ragged floorboards for support. Then strong hands grasped her and she was lifted from the hole and passed to other hands extended from the steps. A moment later Jay was out, too, and standing beside her.

The disintegrating porch was crowded with struggling figures. Someone had leaped over the hole in the floor and was lifting Uncle Frank. Mr. Trelawny was carried out next. Katie heard Joan sob and felt Mrs. Trelawny move away after the rescuers.

"There she goes!"

With a roar, the old house fell in on itself. Sparks rose in a spectacular shower, and a wave of hot air drove the watchers back across the meadow.

"Oh, Katie, what a terrible chance you took! Are you all right? Jay, are you all right?" Mrs. Blaine's face shone with tears in the firelight. "Stay close to me. Please!"

Katie followed to where Uncle Frank and Mr. Trelawny were lying on makeshift mats of jackets and sweaters and robes. She knelt in the grass beside Uncle Frank and touched the flyaway white hair. The hubbub of voices, the crackle of the fire, and the rising wail of sirens seemed far away.

The next day, two memories would remain of the time she knelt there. Once when she glanced up, she thought she saw May Nichols in the crowd, looking down at Uncle Frank with love and concern. As Katie stared, the ghost-girl turned toward her, smiling slightly, and her lips shaped a silent "Good-bye." Then she was gone, and in her place was Jay, his eyes huge and staring in a soot-covered face. One arm hung limp at his side. The other arm supported Katie's mother.

Chapter Seventeen

"You lived there?" The young deputy looked curiously at Katie. She and Joan had backed into the brush to let him drive by, but he stopped when he saw them. "You can look around if you want, but don't go inside the fence. That ground's going to be settling for a long time."

The girls watched the squad car continue its bumpy way back toward town. "I'm not sure I do want to look," Katie murmured, but they walked on through the woods.

Katie stumbled occasionally, because the sneakers she wore were Ed Trelawny's and a size too large. She was wearing a shirt of Ed's, too, and some old blue jeans of Joan's that barely fastened around the waist and were at least three inches too long. The barrette in her hair belonged to Joan's older sister, who lived in Hancock.

Katie had tried to prepare herself for what she would

see, but it didn't help much. Both girls stopped short when they emerged from the woods.

"Wow!" Joan took Katie's hand, and they crossed the yard, ducking under the low-hanging branches of a willow. A snow fence had been put up sometime during the night or early in the morning. Beyond it, wisps of smoke rose where Uncle Frank's house had stood.

They peered over the fence at a sight worse than anything Katie had imagined. Deep cracks in the earth radiated from the pit where foundations, chimney, and scorched beams lay in a blackened jumble. Here and there, recognizable pieces of the house could be seen— a charred door, a window frame, a section of stairs—but most of the pit was covered with ashes. On the far side, a willow, uprooted by the shifting of the ground, lay on its side with yellow-green branches catapulted over the ruin.

"It's like a bomb fell on it," Katie murmured. Most of last night she'd been awake, remembering first one thing, then another, that she wouldn't see again. Her favorite blue sweater with the monogram. Three books from the Newquay town library. The brown loafers that had been new at the beginning of the summer. Her father's lodge pin, and the wristwatch Tom Blaine had given her. The stamp collection Uncle Frank had given to Jay. They were all buried in the pit, along with the chairs and tables and beds, the linen and dishes, the carpets and paintings and the grandfather clock.

"I wish I had—" she began, and then stopped. Was there one thing down there that she absolutely couldn't

get along without? Her mother was safe. Jay was all right
except for a badly bruised shoulder, and the doctor at
Ashland Hospital said Uncle Frank would probably re-
cover after a few days' rest. Mr. Trelawny had regained
consciousness almost at once and had gone to work this
morning. The events of last night had been nightmarish,
but Katie knew she could survive without the things she'd
lost. Uncle Frank was the one who would be heartbroken
when he learned the house was gone.

"Gram wants to come up here and have a look," Joan
said. "She's telling the neighbors she knew it was going
to happen. And my pa's told everybody that your brother's a hero. He says Jay pulled him and your uncle to the
front door when the smoke got so bad they couldn't
breathe. He thinks Jay is one great kid." She turned away
from the pit and drew Katie after her. "I guess I think
he's okay, too. Even though I was mad this morning
when you and he told me about the trick he played on
us. I could have killed him then, but now it seems kind
of funny. I don't mind."

"I don't either," Katie said. And she didn't. The old
resentments and concerns had given way to a quite different feeling. It began when she and Jay had struggled
together to open the front door of the house. They had
been closer right then than they'd ever been before, and
now that it was over, she felt as if they'd passed some
kind of milestone. Uncle Frank had been right when he
told Jay to be grateful just to be alive. It was enough. If
Jay wanted to move out, Katie wasn't going to try to
change his mind. Wherever he went, he would still be

her brother. He'd remember last night, too.

The girls reached the top of Newquay hill and looked down over the town.

"Jay's kind of quiet, though," Joan said. "If I was a hero, I'd be bragging about it."

"It's that barn fire," Katie said. "I think he's really worried. He didn't start it—but what if no one believes him?"

"The sheriff'll believe," Joan said. "Didn't Jay risk his life to save my pa and your uncle? Everything's going to work out, you'll see."

"You sound like the president of the Jay Blaine Fan Club," Katie said. "That's quite a change."

Joan grinned. "Well, I always thought he was cute. Stuck up, but cute. Now that he's a hero I'm willing to forget the stuck-up part."

Katie hoped Joan was right about everything working out. Last night Lillian had given up her bedroom to Katie and her mother, and Jay had slept with Ed. In the tiny, dark room, Mrs. Blaine had whispered that they would return to Milwaukee as soon as they had the sheriff's permission and they were sure Uncle Frank was recovering. "We can't impose on the Trelawnys like this," she'd said. "In a couple of weeks, I'll come back and get Uncle Frank. He'll fight the idea of moving to Milwaukee, but it'll be up to us to make him feel welcome. He and Jay can share a room, I suppose."

Katie wondered what her mother would say when she heard that Jay wanted to leave them. She'd be deeply hurt, but would she stop him? After last night, maybe she, too, would decide Jay had earned the right to make some decisions of his own.

"Look." Joan pointed. Jay and Ed were just starting up from the bottom of the hill. They pulled a coaster wagon laden with groceries.

"Pasty makin's, I bet," Joan commented. "Meat and taters and onions—"

"And beggies," Kate finished. "I know."

They sat on the Trelawnys' steps and watched the boys drag the wagon up the steep slope. "Took you long enough," Joan teased when they reached the front walk at last. Ed made a face at her as he carried two of the bags inside. Jay followed with the third, then returned to sit on the steps beside them, cradling his sore arm.

"Mom's going to see Uncle Frank," Katie told him. "She talked to a doctor on the phone this morning. He'll be okay in a couple of weeks."

"Good deal."

"She's coming back to Newquay to get him later on," she continued. "He's going to live with us. He's going to be p-part of our family."

And then, to her own astonishment, she began to cry. She cried and cried, great hiccuping sobs, while Joan patted her arm and Jay shifted uncomfortably, as if he might be getting ready to bolt. When she stopped at last, she felt relieved, as if something unpleasant but necessary was now behind her.

"Well, I'm glad *that's* over," Jay muttered. "I thought you were going to wash us downhill."

Katie mopped her eyes. "Just because you're a big

hero, you think you're smart."

"Hero! That's a laugh." He tried not to look pleased. "A hero who's maybe going to jail."

"You aren't going to jail," Joan said positively. "No way. My pa won't let you. Besides"—she leaned in front of Katie to peer at him through strands of red-gold hair— "we've got a pretty smart sheriff, even if he is just a hick."

A butterfly danced across the road and lit close to Katie's toe. Butterflies would be part of her Newquay memories, and wildflowers, and meadow winds, and the deer that lived in Uncle Frank's woods. And sitting here on the hill, between her brother and her friend.

"I suppose I could come back on the bus myself and get the old man when he's ready," Jay said carelessly. "Depending on how things go."

Katie took a quick breath. "Mom thinks he won't want to come to Milwaukee," she said. "He won't want to leave Newquay."

Jay shrugged. "He'll come around. What the heck, we're his family now." He jumped up, as if he'd said more than he'd intended. "Hey, what's for lunch, does anybody know?"

"Meat and taters and onions," Joan chanted.

"And beggies," Katie added with a giggle. *My mother and my brother and my uncle and me*—the words rang in her head like the start of a poem. Someday she might figure out the next line, but right now she was too hungry to try.

About the Author

BETTY REN WRIGHT'S short stories have appeared in *Redbook*, *Ladies' Home Journal*, *Young Miss*, and many other magazines. The author of *The Dollhouse Murders* (a 1983 Edgar Award nominee in the best juvenile category), *Getting Rid of Marjorie* and *The Secret Window* (all Apple paperbacks), she has also written 35 picture books. Most of them were published during the years that she was an editor for a children's book publisher. She now devotes herself full time to writing and free-lance editing.

Ms. Wright lives with her husband in Kenosha, Wisconsin.

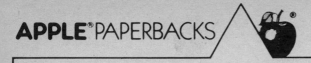

APPLE®PAPERBACKS

Mystery! Adventure! Drama! Humor! Apple® paperbacks have it all!

NEW APPLE® TITLES! $1.95 each

- ☐ QI 32877-8 **Tough-Luck Karen** Johanna Hurwitz
- ☐ QI 33139-6 **Bummer Summer** Ann M. Martin
- ☐ QI 33271-6 **The Telltale Summer of Tina C.** Lila Perl
- ☐ QI 33300-3 **Encyclopedia Brown Sets the Pace** Donald J. Sobol
- ☐ QI 33103-5 **Tarantulas on the Brain** Marilyn Singer
- ☐ QI 33298-8 **Amy Moves In** Marilyn Sachs
- ☐ QI 33299-6 **Laura's Luck** Marilyn Sachs
- ☐ QI 32299-0 **Amy and Laura** Marilyn Sachs
- ☐ QI 32464-0 **Circle of Gold** Candy Dawson Boyd
- ☐ QI 32522-1 **Getting Rid of Marjorie** Betty Ren Wright

BEST-SELLING APPLE® TITLES

- ☐ QI 32188-9 **Nothing's Fair in Fifth Grade** Barthe DeClements
- ☐ QI 32548-5 **The Secret of NIMH™** Robert C. O'Brien
- ☐ QI 32157-9 **The Girl with the Silver Eyes** Willo Davis Roberts
- ☐ QI 32500-0 **The Cybil War** Betsy Byars
- ☐ QI 32427-6 **The Pinballs** Betsy Byars
- ☐ QI 32437-3 **A Taste of Blackberries** Doris Buchanan Smith
- ☐ QI 31957-4 **Yours Till Niagara Falls, Abby** Jane O'Connor
- ☐ QI 32556-6 **Kid Power** Susan Beth Pfeffer

📖 **Scholastic Inc.**
P.O. Box 7502, 2932 E. McCarty Street, Jefferson City, MO 65102

Please send me the books I have checked above. I am enclosing $_____
(please add $1.00 to cover shipping and handling). Send check or money order—no cash or
C.O.D.'s please.

Name_____

Address_____

City_____State/Zip_____

APP851   Please allow four to six weeks for delivery.

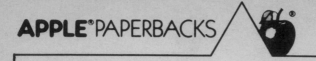